ANSWER IN THE NEGATIVE

HENRIETTA HAMILTON

AGORA BOOKS

ABOUT THE AUTHOR

Henrietta Hamilton is the pseudonym for Hester Denne Shepherd who was born in Dundee in 1920 and was educated at St Hugh's College, Oxford where she earned an honours degree in Modern Languages.

During the Second World War, Hamilton served in the Wrens. Afterwards, she worked in a London bookshop, gaining first-hand experience of antiquarian bookselling – the background of her crime-solving duo, Johnny and Sally Heldar.

During her life, Hamilton enjoyed writing and hill-walking. She died in 1995 in Hastings, East Sussex.

ALSO BY HENRIETTA HAMILTON

ANSWER
IN THE
NEGATIVE

This edition published in 2020 by Agora Books

First published in Great Britain by Hodder and Stoughton 1959

Agora Books is a division of Peters Fraser + Dunlop Ltd

55 New Oxford Street, London WC1A 1BS

ISBN 978-1-913099-48-0

Copyright © Henrietta Hamilton, 1959

Printed and bound in Great Britain by Clays Ltd, Elcograf S.p.A.

CHAPTER ONE

'More coffee, darling?' asked Sally Heldar.

'Yes, please. It seems particularly good tonight.'

'Because we don't always have it,' said Sally, thinking of the price. She refilled Johnny's cup, returned it to him, and sat comfortably back in her chair.

The house was quiet after a busy day. It was a little Regency house in St Cross Square — a peaceful Bloomsbury backwater which had somehow escaped transformation into offices and private hotels. The flat which Johnny had found after the war had been very adequate until they had tried to get Peter into it too. After that they had moved, and the house held the twins and Nanny quite comfortably as well. It was, conveniently, a quarter of an hour's walk from Heldar Brothers' shop in the Charing Cross Road.

The fire was burning well. They had turned out the wall lights and were sitting under the softer glow of the standard lamps. The light fell kindly on the little Adam mantelpiece, the flowered chintzes and the Persian rug, the old rosewood and mahogany pieces which they had inherited from Mark Mercator, who had died by violence four years before. The room was extraordinarily

3

peaceful, and when the front-door bell rang Johnny said wearily, 'Oh, damn!'

But it was no use pretending they weren't in. Anyone who knew them at all knew that there was always someone here in the evening, because of the children. Johnny got up and went out of the room.

A minute or two later Sally heard voices on the stairs. She listened, recognised the second voice, and relaxed just before Johnny opened the door again.

'It's all right,' he said. 'It's only Toby.'

'I hope you mean that kindly.' Toby Lorn looked small and slight beside Johnny. But he was well up to the middle height and by no means puny, though he was always too thin. His hair was dark and smooth, and his cheeks a little hollowed below his horn-rimmed spectacles. He looked tired, as usual. But he smiled and limped forward and kissed Sally affectionately.

'We're delighted to see you, Toby,' she said. 'Have you eaten? There's plenty in the kitchen.'

'Yes, I've eaten, thanks, Sally.'

'Would you like coffee, then — there's lots left — or will you give Johnny an excuse for a drink?'

Johnny looked at Toby's tired face. 'Have mercy on me,' he said. 'I'll get the whisky. Sit down, won't you?'

Toby thanked him and sat down on the sofa, straightening his left leg unobtrusively in its calliper. Toby was the young stepbrother of Peter Lorn, who had been at Porterbury and Magdalen with Johnny and had been killed at one of the Rhine crossings. Young Peter had been called after him. Johnny had found Toby after the war, an unhappy, sensitive sixteen-year-old, recovering slowly and without much enthusiasm from polio, debarred from most public school activities, his father recently dead and his mother clearly not much use to him. Johnny had pulled him through with infinite patience, exercised a certain amount of remote control while he was at Oxford, and seen him into Fleet Street. He was twenty-nine now, still over-sensitive under a professional armour of cynicism — few people guessed that he was the son of a country parson — but standing strongly enough on his own feet and doing pretty well.

Johnny came back with a tray and helped Toby and himself from the decanter and the syphon. They said, 'Cheers,' drank, and settled down again, and for a quarter of an hour or so the room was very quiet. Toby had plenty of conversation when it was needed — with strangers he was apt, like some other newspapermen, to be a slightly feverish conversationalist — but with the Heldars he could relax. Sally, watching him unobtrusively, saw the lines on his forehead smooth themselves out a little. She wondered again if his evening meal had consisted of sandwiches and remembered the bleakness of his flat.

Presently he put his tumbler down and turned to Johnny.

'I'm afraid I really came,' he said, 'because I wanted to consult you.'

Johnny raised an eyebrow. 'Rare book? Manuscript?'

'No. I don't want to consult you as an antiquarian bookseller; I was thinking of your other capacity.'

'Oh,' said Johnny cautiously. 'Don't tell me you've had a murder in Fleet Street.'

'Nothing so interesting, I'm afraid. It's merely a poison-pen in the office.'

Johnny's nostrils twitched a little. 'Not very nice,' he said. 'I'm sorry for you. But poison-pens are rather outside my experience, Toby.'

'I know — at least, I was afraid you'd say so. But will you listen to the story?'

'Certainly.'

'Thank you.' Toby paused to collect his thoughts, and then began.

'I think I'd better explain the set-up first. As you may or may not remember, we're called the National Press Archives. We're a fairly new concern — we only opened six months ago. The Loughbridge Commission on the Press was largely responsible for our foundation, and the Treasury put up part of the money. The object of the exercise was to provide easy access to newspaper cuttings and pictures — photographs and old prints and engravings and so on — for Fleet Street and authors and business firms, and indeed almost anyone. The Fleet Street agencies deposit their stuff with us as soon as its immediate news value has worn off. We make no charge for letting people see a picture or a cutting, but we take a minimum of thirty shillings for any picture which is reproduced. We don't own any copyrights — the agencies didn't want to give them up — so a percentage of the charge goes to the owners. The Archives are divided into two departments, known locally as Feelthee Peex and Comic Cuts, with a Negative Department as a subsidiary to Peex.

'We're housed in the new *Echo* building in Fleet Street. It's a little large for the *Echo*, so they let some of it to us. Peex and Cuts are on the sixth floor, which is the top, and we have basement-room for negatives and messenger boys. You don't want to keep negs in the same place as pix; it's putting all your eggs in one basket, because there's always a risk of fire.'

'I'm putting all my negs in one basket,' murmured Johnny outrageously, with a hint of the Fred Astaire tune.

'Darling, *really!*' said Sally, and Toby groaned.

'Sorry,' said Johnny. 'Couldn't resist it. Go on.'

Toby went on. 'All our printing, and photo-statting of cuttings, is done by the *Echo*'s dark-room — on a business footing, of course. Also, we are allowed to use the *Echo*'s very excellent canteen.' He paused and lit a cigarette.

'So far, the Archives have proved a reasonably successful experiment. But we're not an altogether happy office, principally because we're a mixture of Fleet Street and Civil Service. The Archivist — the man who runs the whole thing — is a Civil Servant. His name is Lionel Silcutt, and the story goes that he was swaddled in red tape at birth. He means extremely well, and he's really rather a nice man. But he can't get on with the present head of Comic Cuts, who is a pure-blooded newspaperman and Irish at that — a man called Michael Knox.'

'The man who wrote for the *Sunday Reflector*?' asked Johnny.

'The same. To my mind he made the *Reflector* — he's a brilliant writer and a brilliant controversialist — and the circulation has dropped since he left. He's an infuriating creature, but Fleet Street will put up with almost any eccentricities in a man who can really write, and I don't think they'd ever have sacked him. He had a stupendous row with his editor about six weeks ago, knocked him down, and walked out. At that time his predecessor in the Archives, who was another dyed-in-the-wool Fleet Street type, had just handed in his resignation because he couldn't get on with Silcutt. Michael thought he'd like the job because he's writing a book and he wanted regular pay and hours which would leave him time for it — and easy access to pix for it. I'm not quite sure why Silcutt thought he would like Michael, but Michael was recommended by James Camberley. It was generous of Camberley, because Mike had just been slating him a bit in the *Reflector*. He's very seldom wrong about a man, and I'm inclined to think still that Mike may have got something —

something for us, I mean. He's still on his month probation — everyone has to do that — and I wouldn't be
surprised if Silcutt gave him a bit longer. To return to
the general set-up — I seem to be wandering a bit — he
has eight assistants and three typists under him.

'The head of Feelthee Peex is me. I can take it —
more or less — because I'm something of a hybrid. I
came to Fleet Street partly because I was still reacting
against a clerical background, and I still like the free-
and-easiness of it. But a year or so ago I began to react
the other way and hanker after discipline and regular
hours. So I took this job when it came along, and on the
whole I like it. I temper it with the odd bit of newspaper work. I have a staff of eleven assistants and three
typists. I am also — rather embarrassingly — set over
the Negatives Department. The staff there consists of
Miss Quimper and four assistants — no typists; they
have very little typing and our girls do it for them. Miss
Quimper is a problem. To begin with she's well over
fifty and I have no right to be set over her. She also re-
minds me vividly of a very devout and strong-minded
church-worker of my childhood who wanted to hear
dear Tobias's catechism every time she came to tea. But
the real trouble is that she was in the old Evans's Picture Library for over thirty years, and although she's
extremely sound in her way she's got immovably set in
it. Her methods are very horse-and-buggy and really
quite impracticable, but she won't modify them, and
when thwarted she bursts into tears.'

'My poor Toby,' said Sally. 'How very upsetting for
you!'

'There is nothing more embarrassing,' said Toby,
'than making a woman cry. It makes one feel like a
monster. To continue, however.'

But he didn't continue at once. He hesitated for a
moment or two. Then he said a little abruptly, 'There's

one other person of importance. A man in Peex called Frank Morningside. He's neither fish nor fowl — neither Civil Service nor Fleet Street — but several other people on the staff are in the same position and don't find it a handicap. He went to a grammar school and a provincial University. A lot of other people went to a grammar school and no University at all, and neither they nor we find it a cause of embarrassment. But Morningside has all sorts of peculiar ideas about public-school types. He was just too young for the war, and did his National Service without distinction, as far as anyone knows. Then, when he'd taken his degree, he taught for several years, and came to this job from that, because he wanted a change. Or possibly because his last job was at a prep school, and he couldn't cope with the brats.'

Toby broke off again. The lines were back in his forehead, and he was concentrating hard — making a sharp effort of some sort. When he spoke again every trace of cynicism had gone from his voice.

'There's nothing wrong with him. He has no vices — I'm quite sure of that. He doesn't drink — except beer; he doesn't smoke, and his life is wide open to anyone who cares to look. He's intoler— he's very smug. He has no sense of humour, but that isn't his fault. He's very good indeed at his job — very steady and methodical. He also has a superb visual memory, which is a great asset in a place like ours. We've taken over a lot of old pix and negs from Evans's and one or two other picture libraries — mostly unidentified stuff salvaged during the Blitz — and he's very clever at spotting well-known people and places in them. He wants to syndicate a sort of "Myself when Young" series — Churchill in a sailor-suit, and Lloyd George in golden ringlets, and so on. The typists call him the Memory Man. There is no doubt that he's an admirable person. There is no doubt that he's a very irritating one, too. But that's no reason for writing him filthy letters.'

There was a short silence. Then Toby went on again, his voice tired now, as if his effort had been a little too much for him.

'It started in a perfectly harmless way, about a month ago. Someone left a rude rhyme on his desk. It was typed on a torn-off piece of office paper. It was quite funny, but not all that clever, and not all that rude either. I can't remember it now. Morningside didn't see the joke. Then he received another, slightly more ribald, but still quite mild, and he was definitely annoyed. And then other things began to happen — silly, irritating things. Someone patronised a joke shop — there's one quite near us, incidentally, in St Barnabas' Lane. Morningside would find blobs of ink on the pix he was going to send out, and they'd turn out to be tin. He opened his desk drawer one day, and one of those snakes on a spring shot out. He plays squash one evening a week and brings a suitcase to the office with a pair of shorts and a sports shirt. One evening when he changed at the courts, he found itching powder in the shorts. And there were other things of the same kind. All very prep school. Meantime the rude rhymes continued and got ruder.

'I should have explained that Morningside has a small private office off Peex. So have I, and so have our typists, and we've always locked our doors at night. Our stuff isn't intrinsically valuable, but it would be tiresome and sometimes impossible to replace. The cleaners come in the morning, and they get duplicate keys from the *Echo* porters' room downstairs. But until this business started not even Morningside, who is extremely conscientious, thought of locking his door when he went to lunch, or when he left his office for a few minutes during the day. But when the persecution got really tiresome, he began to do that. It was hideously inconvenient for everyone else, because clients came in for pix which were in his office, and his telephone rang and no one could answer it, and we wanted his reference books, and so on. But it didn't last long, because it wasn't worthwhile. When his office was locked by day nothing happened. But the things began to happen by night. There was no sign of interference with the lock, so we assumed that the joker had acquired a key. The porters were questioned at once and said that to the best of their knowledge no one but the cleaners had ever had the duplicate. But it seemed quite possible that someone else — almost anyone else — had had it long enough to take an impression, or even to have a new key professionally cut. The porters' room isn't continuously occupied. Since they were questioned one of them has always carried it on him, except when the cleaners have it, but that isn't much good now.

'These investigations were made because Morningside complained to Silcutt. He might have come to me, but he thought I might be responsible for his troubles. Silcutt decided, reluctantly, that he'd better take action. He discussed it with me, and I agreed. We were both inclined to think that either the younger typists in Peex or, more likely, the messenger boys were responsible for the kid-stuff. Silcutt saw the head typist — a nice woman called Mrs Beates — and the two girls, Pat and Pam, who are a little apt to be at the bottom of any trouble. As soon as they understood it was serious, Pat and Pam admitted the two original rhymes. But they persistently denied all knowledge of the rest of it, and Silcutt was satisfied that they were telling the truth. I thought so too. He then saw the boys. There are four of them. Two are probably innocent. The third was christened — or at least registered — Gordon Parston but is known as Teddy because he is a Teddy Boy. He's a crazy mixed-up kid and a hot suspect, and the fourth boy is a buddy of his and easily led. Neither of them would admit anything, but there was a strong presumption of guilt.

'But it wasn't as simple as that. The boys might well be playing about with itching powder. But they were certainly not responsible for the written stuff. It had improved in literary quality, if in nothing else, and was undoubtedly the work of an educated person. Morningside realised that, and thought it was probably Michael Knox's or mine. Or else' — he hesitated a moment, and then went on in a carefully flat voice — 'Selina Marvell's. She's my principal assistant in Peex, and what Morningside would classify as a public-school type. She was also engaged to him recently, and he turned her down — I wouldn't know why. But he thought she might be writing the stuff out of spite.'

So that was it, thought Sally. Toby was in love with this girl with the charming name. That was why he had made his painful effort to be fair to Morningside; he hadn't wanted his portrait to be distorted or obscured by jealousy. He was carrying his passion for integrity in writing over to this story — and probably to his own emotions.

'Here's a sample,' he said, and produced a battered wallet, from which he took a piece of paper. 'One of the earlier ones. Morningside's burnt all the others. He said they were indecent.'

Johnny looked at it. 'No one thought of fingerprints, I suppose. Why should they, after all, at that stage?' He took the paper and read. He grinned once, uncontrollably, and then studied the thing carefully. After a moment he asked, 'Whom did you suspect yourself, Toby?'

'I wasn't sure. I'm still not sure. I don't think Pat and Pam have the intelligence or the literary skill. Selina certainly has.' Toby's voice was still flat. 'It seems a little too hot for her, but one never quite knows. But I thought — and I'm still inclined to think — it was probably Michael. He's quite clever enough, and the ruder stuff didn't start till after he came. And he and Morningside don't get on at all.'

'I see. Let me just get another point clear. Which actually started first, the prep school stuff or the ruder rhymes?'

Toby considered. 'The prep school stuff,' he said definitely. 'I remember because I happened to be with Morningside when the snake popped up, and that was the first incident in this second stage of the campaign. And I think an ink blob appeared before the first of the ruder rhymes, too.'

'Right. Please go on.'

'Well, then the nature of the thing changed again, but gradually this time. The prep school stuff became more serious. Real ink was spilt on Morningside's pix. Then some of them were torn up. Some of the old glass negs he was working on in his leisure moments were smashed. Then his overcoat was slashed. During the same period the ruder rhymes became ruder still, began to give evidence of an ugly mind, and finally degenerated into obscene letters. Here you are. No one thought of fingerprints on them either, I'm afraid.'

Johnny took the dirty envelope, drew out a paper, unfolded it, and read it through. He didn't smile this time.

'Quite so,' he said. 'Rather different from the earlier stuff. Cheap paper — rather cheaper than the other — and cheap envelope, both obtainable at almost any stationer's. Message and name on envelope printed in ballpoint ink, as the rhyme was, but the printing of the rhyme was educated, and this definitely isn't. Still, that doesn't mean it was done by an uneducated person.

One must deduce, I suppose, that it's the effort of a well-educated degenerate.' He paused. 'All these things were left in Morningside's office, I gather, and none of them came by post? Yes.' He restored the paper to its envelope and returned it, with the ruder rhyme, to Toby. 'But, you know, the police could tell you far more about it than I can. Why not the police, Toby? It wouldn't necessarily mean publicity.'

'We're in Fleet Street,' said Toby. 'Everything gets around, and we're not much liked, because we're more or less a government concern. I had quite enough trouble persuading Silcutt and Morningside to let me talk to you. Morningside agreed because he doesn't think its respectable to be involved with the police — and because the letters are driving him nearly out of his mind. Silcutt agreed — finally — because of your amateur status. You could be consulted unofficially — a word which covers a multitude of sins. Even so he had to consult someone else about consulting you. He felt he must take it to a higher level. So I suggested he should talk to Camberley, who of course was on the Loughbridge Commission. As the *Echo*'s Lobby Correspondent, he's in and out of the building a good deal, and he takes an interest in the Archives. He said we must certainly go ahead. I gather he's met you. He gave you a very good Press.'

'That was nice of him,' said Johnny. 'He doesn't really know me — he's an occasional customer of ours. He's interested in anything we can find on North Africa.'

Toby nodded. 'That's his speciality, of course. Well, Johnny, what about it? Do you think you could help us? We should be quite enormously obliged to you.'

Johnny didn't answer at once. He sat frowning at the fire, and Toby waited patiently. He had a curious look of docile resignation — the resignation of a sick person, thought Sally. But his eyes behind his spectacles were anxious.

Johnny turned abruptly. Sally saw his face change a little. Then he said, 'All right. That is, if I'm allowed to ask questions within the Archives.'

'Oh, yes. Silcutt expects that.'

'Good. But I take it you haven't mentioned me to anyone there except Silcutt and Morningside? Then I'd like to sit about for a day or two before anyone else knows what I'm after. Perhaps I could be doing a book on something you've got plenty of stuff on.'

When Toby was really pleased his smile was surprisingly warm and wholehearted.

'That's grand,' he said. 'I'm frightfully grateful, Johnny. The entire collection of Feelthee Peex is at your disposal. We've got a lot of French stuff—' He broke off as Johnny began to laugh. 'All right, all right. I only wanted to suggest something on your own subject.'

'You're only making it worse, Toby dear,' said Sally kindly, and Toby laughed too.

He left them at half past ten, looking a little younger.

Johnny went downstairs with him. When he came back to the drawing room, he looked at Sally and said, 'Do you mind my taking on a job like this?'

'No, I don't,' she said. 'I think poison-pens are things that particularly need to be dealt with. But you weren't going to, were you?'

'No. I thought they ought to go to the police, and it did seem fairly messy. And then' — Johnny sounded slightly exasperated — 'I looked at Toby, and he looked exactly as he did when I first saw him after the war — when he was still a kid and still a bit of an invalid — and I said yes more or less without thinking. I hope it wasn't a mistake.'

'I shouldn't think so. Johnny — I've been wondering

if I couldn't help you with this. If I'd be any use, that is. You can't leave the shop all day, can you?'

'No,' said Johnny, but he looked rather doubtful.

'If you mean you don't think it would be quite nice for me, that's really nonsense, darling. I don't mind.'

'Very well. Thank you, Sally. I'll tell Toby tomorrow that you're sitting in on it. I do feel that we should take the simple and obvious course of noting and recording the people who go into Morningside's office when he's not there. We may get something that way.'

Sally nodded. 'Toby's in love with this girl,' she said irrelevantly.

'The one with the attractive name? Yes, I think so. I hope to God she's not our joker.'

'Is it likely?'

'Probably not. I didn't ask him what she's like, because it would only have embarrassed him, and his opinion is obviously valueless, anyway. We shall just have to wait and see.'

CHAPTER TWO

On the following morning Johnny spent half an hour in the National Press Archives and came home for an early lunch immediately after it. He and Toby had agreed that, as long as he was merely keeping the place under observation, he shouldn't use his own name. It had appeared now in connection with three murder cases, and Fleet Street people were more likely than most to recognise it in that context. He appeared as John Heme — an acquaintance of Toby's, since he had no Fleet Street affiliations and therefore needed some sort of introduction — who was writing a book on English sports. The Archives' resources under this head were practically unlimited, and he could sit over them for hours on end or keep on asking for attention almost indefinitely; clients were not allowed to browse over the files, and all pictures and cuttings had to be got out by a member of the staff. That was one way of getting to know the staff. Not even Morningside himself was to know yet who the Heldars were. Toby said he was a poor actor and had told him only that Johnny was interesting himself in the case.

It was impossible to talk about the case at lunch, which was a communal affair involving Nanny and the children, but Johnny told Sally briefly afterwards that Toby had introduced him to Silcutt, who was very fussed about the whole thing and very reluctant to discuss it, for fear of its becoming too official. Sally's assistance, however, was accepted, and she could go along this afternoon. Johnny himself couldn't; Uncle Charles Heldar had gone down to Kent to look at someone's library, and he was needed at the shop.

Sally removed her wedding ring, put on an old tweed coat, flat-heeled shoes, and no hat, and tried to look like a graduate type. Then she borrowed a blue notebook in which Peter had been drawing pictures, caught a bus to Fleet Street, and walked down the busy pavement to the enormous *Echo* building. There was a window display of good topical photographs. The glass doors in the centre led her into a short hall with lifts on one side, two call boxes on the other, and a reception desk at the far end. The smart young woman at the desk smiled at Sally and said, 'Yes? Who did you want to see?'

'Mr Lorn of the National Press Archives is expecting me,' said Sally. Toby was introducing her as well as Johnny; it didn't matter, he said; he introduced lots of people.

'Sixth floor,' said the girl. 'The lift will take you up.' Sally touched the nearest button and waited, watching the lift's course as indicated by the illuminated numbers above the doors.

Presently it came down, and the doors opened. A tall, fair, ruddy man with a thick moustache was finishing a conversation with the lift-man.

'Yes,' said the lift-man. 'That was a day and a 'alf, sir. What with the 'eat, and the flies, and Jerry givin' us everythink but the kitchen sink — oh, well, it's old days now, sir.'

'Yes, it's old days.' The ruddy man had a pleasant,

deep voice with some sort of country accent below the surface. He smiled, and then he saw Sally and said quickly, 'I'm so sorry.' He came out of the lift, and she noticed that he was unusually straight in the back under his tweed overcoat. His face was vaguely familiar.

The lift-man was obviously thinking about the old days still; he looked preoccupied as he took Sally up. She saw that his left hand was gloved and incomplete. When they reached the sixth floor, she asked him the way, and he pointed to a passage opposite and told her to go down there and turn to her right.

The walls of the second passage were hung with framed photographs. Near the end of it, on the left, was another pair of glass doors. The right-hand door squeaked as she pushed it open.

She walked into a long, wide room furnished principally with dark green steel filing cabinets. The left-hand wall had half a dozen big windows in it, looking out into a well. The nearer stretch of the right-hand wall was broken by three small rooms which stood out into the main one.

A pleasant-looking girl in an unbecoming green frock appeared from nowhere in particular and looked interrogative and welcoming. Sally said, 'Good afternoon. Mr Lorn's expecting me, I think. Miss Merton.' After four and a half years of marriage her maiden name sounded quite unfamiliar.

'Oh, yes, Miss Merton. He said you would be coming in. This is his office.' She turned to the first door on the right. 'Oh, you're there, Mr Lorn. I beg your pardon.'

'It's all right,' said Toby. He was standing in the doorway of his office. 'Good afternoon, Miss Merton. I hope we can be of some use to you. It was portraits of the French royal and noble families before 1789, wasn't it?'

'That's it,' said Sally. 'And some background stuff, if possible. Paris and Versailles, and the *châteaux* of the Loire, and so on.'

'Yes. Well, I think we can offer you something. Come along and we'll see. I asked one of our assistants to leave some stuff out here.'

On the second door was a notice which said, 'Mr Morningside'. The third door was called 'Typists'. Between the two a small table stood against the wall, with a chair in front of it and a pile of pictures on its polished surface.

Toby settled Sally and begged her to apply to him or one of his assistants if she wanted anything more. Then he murmured, 'He's at lunch,' and went back to his own office. Sally opened the blue notebook and spent a minute or two in an effort to interpret the first drawing in it. Peter's technique was slightly surrealist. Finally and rather uncertainly she identified the object as a London bus with unusually fierce headlights and radiator, turned over several pages, and came to a blank one.

She went very slowly through the pile of pictures, making an occasional note. There were photographs of portraits, and original steel engravings, and reproductions of early woodcuts. French social history had always been one of her hobbies, and she found it difficult not to grow too absorbed, the more so since nothing of interest seemed to be happening beside her. Two or three assistants — all women — moved quietly about the composition floor, hunted in the filing cabinets, and talked in low voices to each other or to clients. Clients were taken into Toby's office or settled, like Sally, at tables. At intervals a typist emerged from her office, releasing for a moment the patter of a typewriter, and went off on occasions of her own. Sally had been there for a quarter of an hour or so when one of these girls knocked on the door of Morningside's office with a letter in her free hand and, after a moment, receiving no answer, went in, leaving the door open. Sally glanced at her as she came out, and had a brief impression of a tall, golden-haired, chocolate-box type with something quite unexpected in her wide blue eyes which suggested a sense of humour. Pat or Pam, probably.

Sally returned to her pictures. She was roused a few minutes later by approaching footsteps, evidently in a hurry, and by a violent jar as someone bumped into her table. She looked up in time to see a narrow waist and padded shoulders encased in a black jacket which reached far down over drainpipe trousers of pepper-and-salt tweed. Up above — not very far up — was a bullet head with red hair cut short at the back and brushed into a quiff on top, and a neck which reminded her of Gilbert's dictum about boily boys.

The boy disappeared into Morningside's office. A minute or two later he came out again, revealing a hand-painted tie in the worst possible taste, and said to Sally, 'Hey! Know where old Morny's got to?'

Sally raised her eyebrows. There was a short silence. Then the boy said sulkily, 'Sorry. Do you know where Mr Morningside is — please?' It was clear that his manners had been corrected before, possibly by Toby, who was casual only up to a point. The pseudo-American veneer had gone, laying bare the native Cockney. The pale, freckled wedge of a face under the red hair was, Sally noticed, almost handsome in a sullen, faintly eldritch way of its own.

'I think he's still at lunch,' she said.

The boy made a grimace of annoyance, revealing large, untended teeth. 'Okay. Thanks,' he said, and went away again. Presumably Teddy, she thought, whose real name was something else.

A telephone rang in Toby's office, and she heard him answer it; his door was open.

'Lorn here...You want a dead donkey? I'm not quite sure...Oh, Mr Morningside said he had a dead donkey, did he? Then I expect he's put it aside for you. He's at lunch, but if you'll hold on, I'll see if I can find it.'

He limped up beside Sally a moment later, looking a little harassed, but amused. 'The things people want pictures of,' he said as he passed her.

'The things you've got pictures of, apparently,' said Sally, and he laughed, and went into Morningside's office, and left the door ajar. She saw him hunting through piles of pictures which lay in wire trays on a big table under the window. Then he moved out of her line of vision, and she heard him say, 'Ah!' He reappeared with a photograph and limped back towards his own office.

'Mr Lorn!'

It was a woman's voice, harsh, ugly, too deep. Sally saw her plant herself in front of Toby outside his own door and was astonished that such a deep voice should come from such a tiny creature. She was short and very thin; the only large things about her were her red, bony hands and her enormous brogues. Her small-featured face was pale, and she wore a pince-nez and an indeterminate tweed coat and skirt.

'Miss Quimper,' said Toby politely, 'will you excuse me for one moment? I've got someone on the telephone. Come in and sit down, won't you?'

'I've got to go to Mr Morningside's office,' she said. 'I'll come back, Mr Lorn.'

She clumped along to Morningside's door and into the room. She didn't seem to notice Sally, and like everyone else she left the door open. She moved abruptly about what Sally could see of the office, apparently looking for something on the table and underneath it, and then passed out of Sally's sight as Toby had done. Then she reappeared and stood suddenly still, her face turned away from Sally and towards the window, and her big, ugly, knotted hands twisting and untwisting into one another. Sally looked instinctively down at her pictures. Then she remembered that she was here to watch people. But there was something acutely embarrassing about this middle-aged woman's half-naked emotion. Sally was relieved when she heard the flat sound of Miss Quimper's footsteps on the composition floor and felt her pass close to the little table.

Toby in his office said, 'Right. We'll try to get it round by four-thirty. Yes, the messenger will say it's for you personally. Not at all. Goodbye.'

He came to his door. 'Now, Miss Quimper,' he said. 'What can I do for you?' The Rectory tradition of courtesy to unattractive women died hard, thought Sally.

'Mr Lorn, I really can't put up with this any longer. Mr Morningside has been interfering with my boxes of negs again. If they get out of order I'm hopelessly confused, and it takes me half the day to get straight again. Really I can't go on—'

Sally saw Toby's face of acute distress and heard the tears in Miss Quimper's voice. Toby said gently, 'Come in and we'll talk it over, Miss Quimper.' He stood aside, put a hand on her elbow, and piloted her into his office. Sally was conscious of admiration for him. Then she realised suddenly that she wasn't his only admirer. She saw a girl's face on the other side of the row of filing cabinets which ran parallel with the offices. An exquisite oval face, framed in fair hair, with startlingly dark eyes and a curved, wilful mouth. At this moment the eyes were gentle, and as Sally watched the mouth curled into a warm smile. Then the girl turned away.

Five minutes later Miss Quimper left Toby's office, looking a little calmer. Toby called through the open door of the typists' office, 'Pat, would you mind taking a letter?' and the chocolate-box girl came out with a notebook and pencil and said, 'Of course, Mr Lorn.' Toby held the door of his office open for her, and she smiled at him and led the way in. The smile was frankly provocative, but the look in her eyes made it a sort of family joke.

For a few minutes the life of the place went quietly on. The assistants moved about among the filing cabinets. A client thanked the girl in the unbecoming frock and went away. Another typist came out of the typists' office and vanished.

Then the glass doors squeaked, and a man came in. He was tall and broad-shouldered, and Sally found it difficult not to stare at him, for he was one of the handsomest men she had ever seen. He was middle-aged, but his features were splendid, his eyes dark and fine, his hair thick and iron-grey. Sally wondered who on earth he was.

He walked past her and sidled up to the typists' door. He glanced round it and then half turned, drumming impatiently with his knuckles on the painted wood. Then he moved back to Morningside's door and disappeared through it, shutting it behind him. He came out carrying a big folio and returned to the typists' room.

'Oh, I'm sorry, Mr Silcutt.' One of the typists had come back. 'Did you want a letter taken?'

'Yes, I did.' The voice was precise and rather small, and utterly lacking in authority. 'I rang and no one came. Where have you all been?'

'I'm sorry, Mr Silcutt. Mrs Beates is still at lunch, and Pat is with Mr Lorn. I'll come this minute.' There was a faintly soothing note — perhaps entirely unconscious — in the girl's voice. She hurried into the office, came out with a notebook, and followed Silcutt to the glass doors, and so, presumably, to his own office.

Sally sighed. She couldn't remember ever having experienced such a sense of anticlimax. She knew now why no one had told her that Lionel Silcutt had the head of a great statesman, or a bishop, or a judge. Toby was so accustomed to the little Civil Servant inside that the superb exterior had become irrelevant for him. Johnny must have had her experience — and more forcibly, for he had talked to the man — but he hadn't had time to tell her, and even for him, perhaps, the impact had begun to lose its force. She remembered that he had said Silcutt was fussed. The man Silcutt looked like could never have been fussed. Sally was suddenly and profoundly sorry for him. Nature had played an unkind trick on him.

She was aware of someone who was coming with long strides from the far end of the big room. The footsteps came alongside, and she glanced up again. She saw a very tall, thin figure in a tweed coat and grey flannel trousers in even worse repair than the ones Johnny wore for gardening, and a long head of thick blue-black hair lightly powdered with grey. The tall man went into Morningside's office, drawing the door to behind him, and she heard him moving about inside.

When he came out again her eyes were lowered a little. She saw a scarlet pullover with several darns in various shades of red and several holes, and an emerald-green tie.

'Have you seen Morningside?'

She looked up. 'I'm afraid not. I don't think he's back from lunch.' This time she saw a narrow, high-boned face, with a long mouth and a pair of bright sapphire-blue eyes.

The mouth twisted. 'Always under your feet when

you don't want him, and never there when you do.' He stopped suddenly and seemed to become aware of Sally. 'Your hair is the colour of bracken in the autumn sunlight,' he remarked. His Irish brogue, which had been barely noticeable before, was suddenly much more obvious.

'How very kind of you to say so,' said Sally civilly.

The sapphire eyes danced at her. The long mouth curled in amusement this time. 'You have your wits about you, too,' he said, and bowed to her and strode away.

He had only just gone when a telephone began to ring in Morningside's office. It rang four times, and then someone came running, lightly. Sally saw only a back view again: a tall girl with a very slim figure in a well-cut grey frock, and a beautifully set head with fair hair. Perhaps the girl who had admired Toby's way with Miss Quimper.

Sally heard a click as she lifted the receiver, and then her voice, high, clear, and assured.

'Mr Morningside's office...No, I'm afraid he's at lunch. Can I do anything?...The charge of the Light Brigade?...No, I think it was Balaclava...Never mind; I'll see if he's got anything for you. Hold on, will you?'

A man in an overcoat came quickly past Sally and went through the open doorway into the office. 'Okay, Selina,' he said. 'Who is it?'

'Bruce and Cotton. Charge of the Light Brigade.'

'Oh, yes, they want it to illustrate some advert. I've got something for them here.' Morningside's voice was a flat tenor with some sort of Midland accent which had been carefully and consciously subdued. At this moment it had a tone which Sally found hard to define, or even to analyse. Embarrassment, irritation, a sort of smug condescension, and perhaps, oddly enough, a hint of the defensive. But when he spoke on the telephone, he was sure of himself — or almost sure; his voice was a shade too brisk.

'Hullo. Morningside here. The Charge of the Light Brigade at Sebastopol, wasn't it?'

'Balaclava,' said Selina venomously, and swept out of the room. She didn't notice Sally, but Sally saw her. She was Toby's admirer.

'Yes, I've got something for you,' said Morningside. 'A contemporary engraving and a lithograph in colour. They're not the same picture, but they both show the cavalry charge, and men being hit and falling off, and cannon round about and a lot of smoke and—'

He broke off suddenly. Sally assumed he had been interrupted. But after perhaps twenty seconds he said abruptly, 'Yes, I'm here. Sorry; I — it struck me we might have another picture filed under another heading, but I don't think we have. Shall I send these two along?...Okay, we'll try and let you have them this afternoon...Goodbye.'

He put down the receiver, and there was another silence. Then he came across the room and shut the door sharply. Sally didn't see his face.

A minute or two later one of the typists came to the door: the attractive girl who had taken Silcutt's letter. She had a good figure and a demure expression which might be deceptive. She knocked and went in, and Sally heard her say, 'That's your letter to *Thought*, Mr Morningside.'

'I thought I gave that to Pat,' said Morningside.

'So you did, Mr Morningside. But Pat did half of it and I finished it. It just happened to work out that way. I can read her shorthand.'

'You and Pat — you and Pat—' Morningside's voice rose suddenly. 'You always write everything together, don't you?'

Again there was silence in the office. Then Pam said quietly, 'Mr Morningside, you know—'

'Okay, okay.' His voice was trembling, but under slightly better control. 'I know. I'm sorry, Pam. Thank you.'

'That's all right, Mr Morningside.' Pam came out. Her demure expression was gone. She looked much more adult, and very worried.

Ten minutes later, Morningside himself reappeared. He was a tallish man, fairly well built, wearing a blue suit which was a shade too bright. His hair was mouse-coloured and dry. His features could only be described as ordinary, but his face was distinguished for the moment by a look of angry, haggard misery. He strode out through the glass doors, and a quarter of an hour passed before he came back, looking as unhappy as before. He had barely shut himself into his office when Toby emerged from his and disappeared in his turn. He came back after ten minutes and threw a despairing glance at Sally as he passed her.

For the rest of the afternoon nothing very much happened. People moved about; two or three went into Morningside's office and spoke to him and came out again. Sally knew that, as long as he was there, there wasn't really much point in her keeping watch. But there was always the off-chance that something would turn up. By half past five she knew the pictures on the table by heart.

Between half past five and six the typists and most of the assistants went away, Pat and Pam carrying quantities of letters and packets for the post. At ten minutes to six Toby limped out of his office.

'Have you finished, Miss Merton?' he asked apologetically. 'We're usually closed by six.'

'I'm so sorry,' said Sally. 'I do hope I haven't kept you waiting. What do I do with these?'

'We'll leave them in my office, I think.'

Sally insisted on taking them there herself, but he came with her. He jerked a warning thumb at a glass hatch in the wall between him and Morningside, and said very softly, 'He's had another letter.'

'I was afraid so,' whispered Sally. 'He broke off in the middle of a telephone conversation just after he came back from lunch, and I had the impression he was shaken.'

'He reported to Silcutt, and Silcutt sent for me. I've got the thing now. I'll bring it round, if I may; we can't discuss it here.'

'Do. Come and have a drink.'

'Thank you. I won't leave with you, though. You go ahead. See you presently.'

* * *

SALLY WENT HOME as she had come, and never saw Toby on the way. Johnny was before her, but she got in in time to say goodnight to Peter and the twins. When she went down to the drawing room, she found Johnny and Toby drinking gin and examining the letter.

They stood up as she came in, and Johnny got her a sherry. As he gave her the glass he said, 'Just the same as the other. Same sort of paper and envelope; same sort of ballpoint ink; same sort of printing. Toby says Morningside found it on his desk, under a photograph and a letter typed and presumably left there by Pat, when he came back from lunch a little before half past two. He always goes for an hour or so from about one-thirty. He was talking on the telephone, and fiddling about as one's apt to do, and he uncovered the envelope.'

'He's absolutely certain it wasn't there when he went out,' said Toby. 'You came in just about twenty-five to two, Sally, and about ten minutes after he left. During the first six or seven of those ten minutes I was talking to James Camberley at a point from which I could see the door of Morningside's office, and no one went in except Camberley himself, after a picture. After he'd left, I thought I'd keep a check on the office until you came, if it didn't mean hanging about too obviously. As it happened, you turned up almost at once, and before anyone else had gone in. So if you've got a list of the people who went in after that and before Morningside came back—'

'It's in that notebook beside Johnny,' she said.

Johnny picked up the blue notebook and ran through it.

'Here we are,' he said. '"1.55 Pat" — "or Pam" deleted — "with typed letter".'

'I sorted them out later,' said Sally. 'This one was Pat. Toby, do you know which was immediately on top of this letter, Pat's letter or the photograph?'

'The photograph. Silcutt asked Morningside that. It covered the envelope completely. Pat could easily have put her letter down without noticing the other.'

Johnny continued, '"1.59 Query Teddy. Apparently looking for Mr M."'

'A boily boy,' said Sally, 'with red hair and an incredible tie.'

Toby nodded. 'That's Teddy. He may have been looking for Mr M, and he may have had a perfectly good reason for doing so.'

'Wouldn't he have known,' asked Johnny, 'that Morningside was almost certain to be at lunch at that time?'

'I should have thought so. But it's fair to say that although God gave him some brains, he seldom uses them to any good purpose.'

'Sins of commission as well as omission?'

'Oh, yes. Oh, dear me, yes. He's stayed away without permission on at least eight days in the last six months. I've got him there now, I think, because he's buried three grandmothers. Since he lost count, I haven't had so much trouble; he more or less admitted it was my game. The boys are supposed to come under the *Echo*'s commissionaire for discipline, but it doesn't really work, because he doesn't feel it's his job. That's one reason why we have so much trouble with them. On Guy Fawkes night, for instance, Teddy and the other three lit a bonfire in Garrick Square — that's the little square behind Echo House — and the Fire Service had to be sent for to put it out. The Bench treated that as a sort of Boat-Race Night frolic, but it wasn't all. A fortnight later — last week, indeed — Teddy borrowed a car from the *Echo* park and nearly killed himself and several other people in Holborn. What was more, it turned out to be Camberley's car. He was put on probation for that, and he would certainly have lost his job if Camberley hadn't spoken for him.'

'How old is he?' asked Sally.

'Not quite seventeen. He hasn't got much of a home. His parents don't live together — I don't know if they were ever married — and he lives with an uncle and aunt in the King's Cross neighbourhood who obviously haven't much time for him.' Toby hesitated, and then went on.

'It was the side-door night-porter who rang up the Fire Service on the fifth,' he said, 'and he gave the boys hell afterwards — quite rightly. He's in the habit of having a look round their room after he comes on duty, just to make sure everything's all right, and they evidently knew that. On the evening of the sixth he walked down the steps inside the door and straight into a full fire bucket. He might have damaged himself more than he did.'

There was a short silence. Then Johnny rose and re-filled Toby's glass and his own, and finally returned to the notebook.

'"*2.03 Toby. Looking for dead donkey.*" That is a reasonable thing to look for in Morningside's office, is it, Toby?'

'Eminently,' said Toby gravely. 'I didn't know we had one, but he did. I told you he was good.'

'All right. "*2.05 Miss Quimper.*" Blank. What about that?'

Sally explained, reluctantly, and Toby looked unhappy.

'It was her negs again,' he said. 'These boxes of glass negs from Evans's and the other defunct agencies. She arranges them all very carefully, because she likes to file the ones we keep in a certain order, and therefore Morningside must examine them in a certain order and return those he doesn't reject in that order. Once when he couldn't get two boys to bring a box up, he went down himself and took one with Teddy, and it was the wrong one, and she raised hell. She thought this afternoon he'd been messing up another box, and she said he'd taken some of the already filed stuff too. I promised I'd tackle him, but I haven't done it yet, because he was so upset about the letter. It's quite possible he isn't responsible this time. One of the boys may have done it only to annoy — most likely Teddy. I'm not sure, though, because whoever it was borrowed a pair of the cotton gloves, they always use to handle negs, and I doubt if Teddy would have bothered with that.'

'You say it takes two boys to shift the things?' asked Johnny.

'It takes two boys to get them upstairs, even in the lift. Morningside can heave them about in his office. Miss Quimper can lift them about a bit, too; she's astonishingly muscular, considering her size. It's partly practice, of course; she's been doing it for over thirty years.' He hesitated again, and Sally saw in his face the familiar reluctance, and the familiar determination to leave nothing unsaid. 'She resented it very much when Morningside was asked to go through the negs. She thought they were her job — particularly the ones from Evans's, because she worked with them there. But we couldn't have let her do it. She'd never have rejected anything, and we haven't room for anything like all of them. Most of them are so much lumber, anyway — the local grammar school hockey team in 1924, and so on. And, anyway, she hasn't got Morningside's memory. I did my best to calm her down this afternoon, but it wasn't easy.'

'Did she say why she was in Morningside's office?' asked Johnny.

'I don't think she did. She said she'd got to go there. I assume she wanted to check up in case he'd taken any negs.'

'She said she'd got to go to his office, not to see him? In other words, she knew he would be at lunch?'

'She said she'd got to go to his office, yes.'

'Right. *"2.18 Mr Silcutt. Came out with large red folio."*'

'That would probably be a bound volume of old magazines,' said Toby. 'Early *Graphics*, or something. He might want them almost any day, almost any time. Though I'd expect him to ring through and send a typist for them.'

Sally explained the temporary lack of typists, and Toby nodded and said, 'Fair enough.'

'"2.21",' said Johnny. '"*Query Michael Knox. Apparently looking for Mr M.*"'

'A long, lanky Irishman?' asked Toby. 'Yes, that's Michael. He could have been looking for Morningside as well as anyone else. It might have been a purely professional matter, or it might have been pix for his book.

33

He was a war correspondent, and he wants stuff on France and North Africa. He wants it badly and quickly — though I can't quite see why it's so urgent — and he takes rather too much advantage of his position in the Archives. It irritates Morningside very much, and Michael knows it and usually picks on him when he wants anything.'

'But surely he'd know Morningside was at lunch?' asked Johnny.

'He'd know if he thought about it. As like as not he wouldn't think.' Again Toby hesitated, and again went firmly on. 'He doesn't care for Morningside — they're very obviously as different as they could possibly be. Morningside is' — Toby frowned, searching for phrases that would be scrupulously fair — 'he's a narrow man — a typical suburbanite without any experience of the world — a good man because he's never really come into contact with evil, and from Michael's point of view quite unjustifiably smug about it. That's probably,' said Toby parenthetically and half to himself, 'why he sees evil where there isn't any, and probably wouldn't know it if he really did see it. Sorry; I'm wandering. Michael, on the other hand, has seen ten times more of the world than any of us, and knows more about human nature in all its aspects than ten slum padres and ten policemen put together. He's extremely tough, in the real sense of that misused word, and he has many faults — selfishness, of a kind, among them. And he has no patience with — with untried virtue. So they're at daggers drawn all the time.'

Johnny nodded, and glanced down at the notebook again. "*2.25 Query Selina Marvell. To answer telephone.*"

'A girl like a Gainsborough,' said Sally.

'That's Selina, yes,' said Toby to his glass.

'She answered the telephone, but Morningside came

in while she was still there and took over, and she came out again.'

'Well, that would seem to be all,' said Johnny.

'Any ideas?' asked Toby.

'Plenty of ideas milling around, but they're no use till they're sorted out — if then.'

'I'm sorry. I'll leave you to it. I'm meeting a man at the Magpie and Stump at a quarter past seven.'

'I don't think you are. Not now,' said Johnny. 'It's nearly ten past.'

'Damn. I must just be late, then. Thank you for the drinks. Goodnight, Sally. See you tomorrow, I hope.'

* * *

JOHNNY OFFERED TO COOK SUPPER; Sally said she could very easily do it, and, in the end, they made it a joint effort. But Johnny hadn't much to say. He was obviously thinking about something else, and Sally had to take over when the omelette was half cooked, because his mind was not on the job. He apologised rather vaguely and began to cut some bread which they didn't want. Sally told him that if he wasn't careful, he would get like Uncle Charles, whose vagueness was a byword in Heldar Brothers, and he grinned and pulled himself together a little. But he was rather silent over the meal and over the washing-up, and though Nanny didn't have supper with them, it was only when they had returned to the drawing room that he really surfaced and returned to the case. He lit his pipe slowly and carefully, and then asked, 'Did any of these people who entered Morningside's office while it was empty seem to you to spend an undue time there? We can check that to some extent from your timetable. Let's take them in order. Pat first.'

Sally thought carefully. 'She went in and came straight out again.'

Johnny made a note in the blue book. 'All right. Teddy?'

'Teddy — of course, if Teddy was only looking for Morningside, he had no reason to go in at all. He need only have put his head round the door. He should have knocked, of course, but he didn't. Perhaps he was just inquisitive. He was inside for a minute or two, and I couldn't see what he was doing.'

'Right. Toby?'

'You don't suspect Toby?'

'Not seriously, Sally. But remember, we're looking for someone who is probably unbalanced, and that means someone who might conceivably have called us in when he himself was guilty. In any case, we've got to consider everybody.'

'Very well, darling. Toby was looking for dead donkeys. It took him about two minutes, and I could see him for most of that time.'

'Then Miss Quimper went in as soon as he came out?'

'More or less. She was in for about two minutes, too, and in my sight for part of the time. I — I wasn't watching her very carefully, anyway.'

'Silcutt?'

'Silcutt went straight in and out again, but he shut the door behind him. Michael Knox was next, wasn't he? He had no reason to go in if he was just looking for Morningside. He shut the door behind him, and he was there for a good two minutes — perhaps three. I suppose he may have been looking for his pictures. And Selina Marvell was last. She was talking on the telephone all the time she was there till Morningside came in.'

'Yes,' said Johnny slowly. 'I don't think, you know,

we can allow any one excuse for being in Morningside's office to satisfy us more than any other. The joker may have thought it wise to have a sound one; he may have argued that anyone who was interested would look for a visitor with a sound one, and therefore left it a bit vague, or he may have waited till circumstances forced him into the office. After all, there was no particular hurry, and he — or she — could always have the letter ready for an impromptu visit. Incidentally, Sally, you seemed a little unforthcoming about Selina's visit. I had the impression we were only getting the bare bones of it.'

'Yes,' said Sally, and told him the rest of it. He listened thoughtfully.

'Funny little scene,' he said. 'I can't imagine how those two came to be engaged. Can you?'

'Not really. Perhaps she mistook his untried virtue for tried strength. Perhaps it was a genuine mistake, or perhaps she just wanted a solid prop and persuaded herself she'd found it — poor girl.' Sally smiled a little, looking at Johnny, knowing that she had made no mistake.

He nodded slowly. 'And in that mood the middle-class virtues might seem very desirable,' he said.

'Johnny, are you putting your money on anyone yet?'

'No,' he said. 'Not yet.'

CHAPTER THREE

Johnny spent the next morning in the Archives and came home at midday again. It had been, he said after lunch, a rather unprofitable visit. Morningside had remained in his office all the time and had been irritable with everyone on the staff who had spoken to him in Johnny's hearing, and barely civil to two or three clients. Johnny himself had made an excuse to talk to Selina Marvell, whose late engagement still puzzled him, and said she was intelligent and charming, but he hadn't got beyond the intelligence and charm. He had also penetrated to Comic Cuts, another long room beyond the first, and talked to Michael Knox, whom he thought brilliantly clever, extraordinarily interesting, and probably quite amoral. And that, he said, was all he had to report.

Sally reached the Archives, as before, a little after half past one. For the moment there seemed to be no one about, and she knocked on Toby's door, found him at home, and asked if she might collect her pictures.

'Certainly,' said Toby, rising from behind his desk. 'Come along in, Miss Merton.' She shut the door, and he added under his breath, 'Morningside hasn't gone out. He's in such a state that he won't leave his office. He wouldn't have had any lunch, but Pat got him some sandwiches from the canteen.'

'Oh, dear,' said Sally.

'It is unfortunate. Well, I don't know what you can do but wait and see.'

Sally waited, and for most of the afternoon saw very little. Not very many people went into Morningside's office, and with those who did, as far as she could hear, he was short. The time passed slowly, and no one of interest appeared. It was just before five o'clock when Teddy and a short boy came past her, carrying a stout wooden box, about twenty-four inches by nine, full of glass negatives stacked on edge. The boys crashed into the office without looking, taking some paint off a jamb, and Morningside's voice said, 'For heaven's sake take care what you're doing, you clumsy clots. No, don't put it on that shelf; it won't take it. And not on those negs — you'll break them. Teddy — put that box down and get out!'

'Okay, okay. Keep yer shirt on,' said Teddy. The box was dropped on the floor, and Morningside broke out again. The other boy came out of the office, looking rather worried. Teddy said, 'All right, mister. Wotcher goin' ter do abaht it? That's wot I wanter know. Wotcher goin' ter do abaht it?' The unmistakably Cockney voice was eager, almost anxious.

'I don't know,' said Morningside. His voice was trembling with anger. 'I haven't decided. But if you go on this way, you'll get what's coming to you, you little—'

Teddy got his epithet in first, and left the room, slamming the door behind him. His freckles stood out almost startlingly on a dead white face. He said harshly to the other boy, 'Come on, Bill,' and strode away to the glass doors, with Bill behind him. As he reached them, they opened, and the big, ruddy man whom Sally had seen in the lift yesterday afternoon came in. Teddy stepped quickly aside. The big man smiled, and then stopped and looked at him. Teddy stood still — almost, to Sally's astonishment, at attention.

'Anything wrong, Parston?' asked the big man.

'No, sir,' said Teddy flatly.

'All right. By the way, have you got another tie at home — a quieter one?'

'Yessir.'

'Then I should wear it at the office. That one really won't do. Wear it at home if you must, but not here. All right?'

'All right, sir.'

'Fine.' The ruddy man nodded to Bill, who had come to attention nearby, and walked on. He recognised Sally, who hadn't returned to her pictures in time, and smiled and nodded again. She smiled back, and he stopped beside her and knocked on Morningside's door. Morningside called sharply, 'Come in,' and the ruddy man opened the door and put his head round it.

'Have you by any chance got me those desert pictures?' he asked in his pleasant voice. 'It doesn't matter if you haven't had time; I was just passing and thought I'd look in.'

'Yes, I've got them, Sir James. Please come in. I hope they'll do.' Morningside spoke much more calmly.

So that was Brigadier Camberley, thought Sally. His face had seemed familiar yesterday; she had seen his photograph in the newspapers more than once. He looked a nice man, and he seemed to be effective.

He came out of Morningside's office a few minutes later, carrying a large, well-filled envelope, and moved on to Toby's. He knocked and disappeared inside.

Five minutes passed. The big room was quiet. No one else visited Morningside, and he didn't come out.

When the interruption came, it almost startled her. Michael Knox swung suddenly past her table. He didn't notice her, and he didn't knock at Morningside's door. He walked straight into the office and said loudly, 'Have you got those Tunisian pix?'

'I wish you wouldn't walk in without warning like that,' said Morningside crossly.

'Why? You haven't got Selina on your knee.'

'That's a disgusting suggestion!' Morningside's voice was almost a scream. 'You know I—'

'You wouldn't do that in the firm's time?' Knox leaned against the jamb, his hands in the pockets of his disreputable coat.

'I wouldn't do it at any time. Now—'

'No, it's not done in Balham, I suppose.'

'I suppose you think that's funny,' said Morningside shrilly. 'Well, let me tell you I don't understand public-school humour. I went to a grammar school. I don't think it's funny to talk like that and bandy about a lady's name in public.'

'That's a real gem,' said Knox delightedly. 'In the very best Victorian tradition.'

'You're not writing now, Knox. I won't—'

The high voice broke off suddenly. There was a moment's silence. Then Morningside said in a quite different voice — flat and expressionless and rather dull, 'So it is you who's writing the letters. That's just the sort of thing you say in them. About Selina—' His footsteps sounded flatly on the composition floor.

'Take it easy,' said Knox calmly. His hands were still in his pockets.

'I won't take it easy.' Morningside was directly in front of Knox now, standing in the doorway, side-on to

Sally, and entirely unaware of her. His voice rose again. 'I won't have you saying things about Selina.' He raised his clenched fists in what looked even to Sally a rather clumsy and amateurish way.

Knox's hands came out of his pockets so quickly that she scarcely saw them move. The long bony fingers closed round Morningside's wrists, and he looked suddenly helpless.

'Don't be a bloody fool,' said Knox contemptuously. 'I don't want to hurt you. And it's you who are saying things in public, not me, you know.'

Sally became suddenly conscious that Toby was standing beside her. How much of all this he had heard she didn't know. The blood was in his thin face.

'It sounds to me as if neither of you were showing to much advantage,' he said, and his voice cut like a lash. 'You might break it up now. There are clients here, and the Brigadier is with me.'

Knox made a sound of disgust which was pure Irish, dropped Morningside's hands, and swung out of the room. Sally caught a whiff of whisky as he passed her. That probably explained something of this scene. He must keep a flask or a bottle in his office; the pubs were barely open yet, even in Fleet Street. Morningside stood quite still for a moment, his released hands at his sides, and a look of despair on his uninteresting face. Then he shut his door. Toby turned and limped back to his office. His shoulders were rigid.

Just before half past five the Brigadier went away. Sally waited another quarter of an hour or so, just in case anything more happened, and saw most of the staff leave. Toby went into Morningside's office, knocking first, and shut the door behind him. She hoped he wouldn't be long; it would be better to see him before she left. She was putting her pictures together when she heard someone walking with long strides behind the filing cabinets. The footsteps halted suddenly, and Michael Knox's voice said, 'Come and have a drink, Selina.'

'Not tonight, thank you.' Selina's voice was lowered, but still clear, and very cold. 'You've had more than enough already, Mike.'

'If I didn't have a drink or two now and then I couldn't stand this bloody place.'

'It probably won't stand you much longer. Must you pick quarrels with everyone?'

'I must. It's my cursed nature.' His brogue had cropped up again.

'Stop going all *Juno and the Paycock*,' snapped Selina. 'It may be very effective with complete strangers, but I know just how bogus it is.'

Knox was silent for a moment. Then he said very softly, 'All right, Selina. In that case you know just why I have to quarrel with Morningside.'

There was another short silence. Then a chair skidded on the floor and Selina whispered furiously, 'No. No, Mike.'

Again there was silence. Then Knox said in a low, hard voice, 'All right. Not tonight, then. But, by God, I won't believe you prefer that bourgeois from Balham to me.'

Selina said on a note of faint surprise, 'You're quite wrong—' But Knox had gone. He strode on to the glass doors and went out without looking back. Presumably he had finished for the day, but he wore no overcoat.

Sally sat still for a minute, rather unhappy. She was here to watch and listen, but she hadn't quite reckoned on this sort of thing. She wondered if she could possibly get away without Selina's realising she was still here.

Toby dashed that hope. He came out of Morningside's office and said, 'Oh, you've finished, have you, Miss Merton? I think we'd better put your stuff away.'

He followed her into his own office. He was looking very tired, but not quite as wretched as she had expected.

'Sorry about that sordid scene,' he said quietly. 'Not to edification, as my father used to say about the lower forms of newspaper life. Look, Sally. I think something's got to be done about Morningside. If we can't relieve the tension a bit, he'll crack. You've seen for yourself the state his nerves are in. He's not sleeping, and when I offered him some dope, he said he didn't approve of taking drugs. He's not eating. He nearly always works late on his negs on Wednesday evenings, and has supper in the canteen. He said he wasn't going down this time, only Camberley persuaded him to do it. He's afraid to leave his office, in case the joker looks in. As far as I can see there's nothing to prevent him from working all night — a newspaper building doesn't shut.'

'I can see he's on the edge of a breakdown,' said Sally. 'But we've got to give Johnny time.'

'I know. I was only going to suggest that Johnny should talk to him tonight. If you want to carry on with this observation after that, then he must just take a day or two off, so that he can't give you away. If no one knows how long he's to be off, the chances are the joker won't suspend his activities. Do you think Johnny will agree?'

'That's up to him. You'd better come along and ask him.'

'I can't, Sally. I'm meeting Camberley for a drink. Supposing I ring Johnny up. Will he be home by now?'

'I don't know, but I should try it before the shop.'

Toby dialled the Heldars' number. Evidently the Archives had their own telephone system, and no connection with the *Echo's*. After a minute Johnny answered. Sally could hear only one end of the conversation, but she gathered that he agreed. Toby said, still softly, 'No, I think eight o'clock should be absolutely all right. I'll meet you down in the entrance hall…Yes, I'll send her home now.'

He put down the receiver, and Sally said, 'Toby, I hope you're going to have a proper meal.'

'Oh, yes. I shall probably go to the canteen. Camberley won't want to linger over his drink; he's eating early, I gather, and going on to the House. Middle East debate.' Toby broke off and glanced at his watch. 'It's nearly six. I'm supposed to be meeting him downstairs, and I promised Johnny I'd send you home at once. Come along.'

As he opened one of the glass doors for her, a door at the end of the passage opened too. Camberley and Silcutt came out. Camberley grinned and said, 'Hullo, Lorn. I've been gossiping ever since I left you, I'm afraid.'

Or possibly soothing Silcutt, thought Sally. Toby said, 'The day's work is over, sir. Even for the Archives. Sally, may I introduce Sir James Camberley and Mr Silcutt?' His voice dropped slightly. 'This is Mrs Heldar.'

Silcutt looked faintly embarrassed, as if he would have preferred to ignore the existence of unofficial adjuncts to detection, and murmured something incoherent, but Camberley said, 'We've almost met, Mrs Heldar, though I didn't know who you were.' He shook hands with a grip that was hard without being painful. 'It's extraordinarily kind of you to help us with this nasty business. Tell me, can you spare the time to join us for a drink? Mr Silcutt says he must get home, but Lorn and I are on our way to some respectable bar.'

Sally liked the warmth of his deep voice. It would have interested her to see more of him. But she must say goodnight to Peter and the twins, and she was much more anxious to see more of Johnny than of any other man. She explained that she had a family, and Camberley smiled and didn't press her.

'I hope you and your husband will join me another evening,' he said, and it sounded as if he meant it.

They all went down in the lift together. On the pavement they said goodnight, and Camberley and Toby turned left. Silcutt bolted away to the right, and Sally followed more slowly, but still briskly. She caught up with him at the corner of St Barnabas' Lane, where he was getting into a taxi. He didn't see her. She heard him give his destination in his small, precise voice.

* * *

WHEN SHE GOT HOME Johnny was peeling potatoes in his shirt-sleeves. He put down the peeler and kissed her, and she held on to him for a moment and said, 'I've been thinking all afternoon about coming home and finding you here. It is silly, isn't it? After so long.'

'Very silly,' he agreed gravely, and gathered her more tightly against him. 'Now you know how I feel every afternoon.'

After a minute or two she said, 'I must go up and say goodnight. I shan't be long. We ought to eat at seven, I suppose.'

'Or soon after,' said Johnny.

When she came down again, they sat at the kitchen table, while the potatoes boiled and the chops grilled, and she told him the story of the afternoon. When she came to the scene between Morningside and Knox, he nodded. 'Yes,' he said. 'Selina was mentioned in both the letters I saw. Not by name, but unmistakably.'

Sally went on to the scene between Knox and Selina,

and he frowned a little. 'Do you suppose he's really in love with her?' he asked.

'It's difficult to say. But I think from his point of view he is. Do you think he is responsible for the letters?'

'I don't know, my darling.' Johnny got up and prodded the potatoes with a fork, and then sat down again.

'I want to get this clear in my mind,' he said, 'before I see Morningside.' He paused, frowning again, to collect his thoughts.

'The items in the persecution of Morningside can be divided into several categories. The first of them — chronologically — were two rude rhymes, which were evidently left in his office while it was unoccupied but open. On their own admission, Pat and Pam were responsible for that. On their own statement, they were not responsible for any of the items in the second and third categories — the prep school stuff and the ruder rhymes. If we accept that statement, and if we can decide that they are not responsible for the fourth and fifth categories — the really serious stuff — we can assume that the two rude rhymes are unimportant in themselves, and to be considered only in so far as they may have given ideas to someone else.

'The second category, as I said, consists of the prep school stuff — tin blobs of ink, itching powder, and so on. I fancy that particular problem is now solved. I paid a visit this morning to the joke shop in St. Barnabas' Lane which Toby mentioned. It sells Meccano and Dinky toys and suchlike, as well as joke stuff, and the proprietor is an aged professional humourist. I got what I wanted, though. I explained that I was working in an office where one of the messenger boys was suspected of a joke campaign which was upsetting everyone very much. If it couldn't be quietly and unof-

ficially stopped, he would probably lose his job. I described Teddy, and the old man told me at once that he
had been a regular customer for about ten days at the
beginning of this month and hadn't been back since. He
had sometimes been accompanied by a short boy, who
was, I should think, Bill. He had bought itching powder,
ink blobs, a snake on a spring, and so on. He's not quite
a usual type, so it isn't very surprising that he was remembered. I bought a Dinky tractor for Peter, and the
proprietor and I parted the best of friends.

'I think we may assume that Teddy, with Bill as his
accomplice, was responsible for the prep school stuff,
and that after Silcutt's interrogation he decided to let
up on it. If we could be sure he was responsible for
nothing else, we could also assume that these items
again are important only in so far as they may have
given ideas to someone else. It's very improbable, you
see, that Morningside inspired three entirely indepen-
dent and coincidental persecutions. It's possible that
Pat's and Pam's efforts and Teddy's were separately inspired — I admit Morningside was a natural for that
sort of thing — but equally possible that Teddy heard
about the rude rhymes, thought them a good idea, and
produced a sequel more suited to his intelligence quo-
tient. In any case, three separate inspirations are too
many.

'The third category consists of the ruder rhymes.
Morningside was receiving them at the same time as
Teddy's attentions, but Teddy's attentions started first.
Teddy was certainly not responsible for the ruder
rhymes; they were a long way above his head or Bill's.
The one I saw showed a very considerable degree of intelligence and skill, and some acquaintance with the
less well-known poets. I talked to Pat and Pam this
morning, and I agree with Toby that they're not up to
the required standard. Toby is practically certain that

most of the staff of Peex, Negs, and Cuts can be dismissed — as far as the rhymes are concerned — on the same grounds. But we're left with several people. Michael Knox, who wasn't there, I gather, at the time of the original rude rhymes, but could easily have heard about them; Selina Marvell; possibly Miss Quimper, who is an educated woman, though she doesn't appear to have much sense of humour, and Toby himself — Toby being the least likely, because if he were responsible for the ruder rhymes and not the filth he would probably have told me, and if he were responsible for the filth as well he probably wouldn't have called me in. But one can't be sure about that.'

'What about Silcutt?' asked Sally. She had turned the chops and was prodding the potatoes again.

'Silcutt? Yes, I suppose one ought to include him. Though he doesn't seem to have any sense of humour either. To continue: we must note that during this stage of the persecution someone acquired a key to Morningside's office. Almost anyone, as Toby explained, could have acquired a key, and we can assume that it was done either by Teddy or by the rude rhymester. That's an important point, for if we knew who had acquired the key, we should know who was responsible for the letters. Most of them are delivered by night, and therefore by someone who has a key. It can scarcely be a new joker inspired by example to acquire a key, because the porters' duplicate hasn't been available since the first copy was taken. We can't rule anyone out on any grounds other than these. The letters don't demand brains or skill or knowledge. This third stage in the persecution may of course be another divided effort. It may be that Teddy is responsible for the poltergeist stuff — tearing up pictures and smashing negatives and so on — and the unknown joker is responsible for the letters. Or, of course, Teddy may be responsible for the whole lot. I haven't quite gathered yet whether the poltergeist stuff happens by day or by night, or both. I'll get that straight with Morningside this evening. But the other point is more important. If he can say for certain that only the prep school properties or only the ruder rhymes were delivered at night, we shall be at least a step farther on. We may even be home, because we shall know whether Teddy or one of the other four — no, five — is our joker.'

'Darling!' said Sally. 'I'd no idea you were anything like so near home.'

'I don't know how near we are, Sally. Morningside may not be quite clear about the things himself. He's said to have a good visual memory, but that's not quite the same as a memory for events. Still, I think we can probably sort it out. But we may well find ourselves faced with the choice between Knox and Selina and Miss Quimper and Toby.'

'And Silcutt,' said Sally, dishing up the potatoes.

'And Silcutt. Odd how one forgets that magnificent man. And, Sally, there's always Morningside himself, you know.'

'Yes. I did think of that. We know he isn't responsible for the rude rhymes or the prep school stuff, and I don't suppose he'd be up to the ruder rhymes, but could all that have suggested the rest of it to him? Consciously or subconsciously?'

'I wouldn't know at all. I must try to find out.'

Nanny came down, stout and comfortable and starched, and collected her supper. She was of the old-fashioned type, and a little apt to treat Johnny and Sally as if they had been her charges too, and not so long ago, either, but they reckoned her one of their greatest blessings. They suspected that she felt the shop to be a slight stigma, but otherwise they seemed to measure up to her rigid standards.

They had reached the cheese when Sally said, 'By the way, do you want me to come with you, or would it be better not?'

Johnny opened his mouth to answer, and then changed his mind and considered the question. After a minute he said, 'I was going to say better not, because it would probably embarrass Morningside. But on second thoughts I believe I'd like you to come, if you wouldn't mind. You might as well meet him. But the point is, Sally, that unless the joker is Toby, he doesn't know there's going to be a conference, and he may try to do his stuff this evening. These offices aren't quite sound-proof, and it's unlikely he'll get as far as walking in on us. But if there were someone next-door to keep a look-out for him — would you simply hate it, darling? I'd post Toby, but I want him in on the conference.'

'I'll do it, of course.'

Johnny looked worried. 'You'll have to be in the dark.'

'I don't mind that.' She didn't like any of it much — the dark, the great empty room with the rows of filing cabinets throwing shadows to hide anyone who came, the waiting for someone who was probably not quite sane — she remembered Michael Knox's hard bony fingers. Then she remembered Morningside's helpless despair, and said, 'No, of course I don't mind. You'll be within call.'

Johnny put his big hand over hers where it lay on the table and held it for a moment. 'I shouldn't dream of suggesting it otherwise,' he said. 'We'll put you in Toby's office, with the door open. As soon as anyone passes it, you turn on the light and scream. If he goes back the way he came he'll have to pass the lighted doorway. On no account try to stop him; just see who he is.'

'And if he comes in the other way? Or can't he? Is

there any way in through Comic Cuts? I can't very well explore those parts; there wouldn't be any cuts on my subject.'

'Plenty on mine. Yes. The doors at the far end of Peex lead into a short passage. There's a Ladies' and a Gents', and then a lift and a staircase, and Cuts at the far end. If you hear footsteps approaching from that direction, give it as long as you dare and then light up and scream, if possible, before he turns back. He can't break sideways, that's one thing; the filing cabinets will stop him.'

Sally nodded and looked at her watch. 'It's just after half past seven,' she said. 'Have we time to wash up, or not?'

'I should think so, yes. There isn't very much, and we're going to be devils and have a taxi.'

The telephone rang. Johnny sighed and went out to answer it in the hall. Sally stacked the dishes on the draining board and began to wash. She had just emptied the bowl and picked up a towel when he came back.

'Ah!' he said. 'I seem to have timed that rather neatly.' He sat down at the table and leaned complacently back in his chair.

Sally hung the towel over his shoulder, urged him on to his feet, and sat down in his place. He groaned and began to dry, and she said callously, 'And who was it?'

'Toby. He told Camberley we were having this conference, and Camberley said he'd very much like to sit in on it. But he didn't want to force an audience on me if I preferred to be without one, so he asked Toby to ring up and make sure I didn't mind. I don't, of course. He's just the man we want, if Morningside's going to be jittery. The two of them and Toby have just been eating in the *Echo* canteen. Morningside was evidently not frightfully pleased when Toby broke it to him that we'd been detecting without his knowledge, but the Brigadier smoothed his ruffled feathers, and he's quite relieved by the idea of the conference. I said you were coming, though you wouldn't be in on it, and Toby said that would be fine.'

Sally nodded and hoped that Toby was right.

CHAPTER FOUR

I t was a dark night, and a thin rain had begun to fall. They drove to within a hundred yards of Echo House and walked from there along the wet pavement. Johnny kept Sally's arm in his. It was two minutes to eight by the rather indistinct contemporary clock above the reception desk when they came into the entrance hall. There was a porter at the desk now, not a girl. Night-shift, thought Sally.

Toby was sitting on a red quilted seat — a modern version of Edwardian plush — which ran along the left-hand wall between the call boxes. Beside him, large and reliable, was the Brigadier.

They stood up, Toby a little awkwardly, as usual. He mentioned no names, probably because of the porter. He said only, 'Ah, here you are. Come along,' and led the way, firmly, to the farther of the two lifts. When it came down Sally thought she saw his reason. There was no lift-man in it; perhaps the night-shift didn't provide for one.

As soon as they were in the narrow, enclosed space and moving gently upwards, Camberley held out his hand to Johnny.

'We've met at Heldar Brothers,' he said. 'I'm very

glad to see you. I think we need you badly. I fully admit I've no right to be here, and I ought to be at the House, but I should be enormously interested to hear what you make of the case. Are you quite sure you wouldn't rather be left to get on with it, though?'

'I shall be very glad if you'll come, sir,' said Johnny. 'I gather Morningside wants a bit of handling.'

Camberley looked at him and said, 'You can do that, I think. He's looking forward to meeting you.'

'He's an extraordinary man,' said Toby. 'When he grasped that you and Sally were the people who'd been sitting about outside his door for the last two days he said, "Of course. I ought to have known. I thought I recognised them. I connected them with some pix of an inquest in Hampshire that we took over from Dale's." I take it he was right?'

'Yes,' said Johnny. 'It would be one of the Westwater murders.'

The lift stopped, and they walked out of it. They made surprisingly little noise on the composition flooring. Johnny's step was always astonishingly light; his Commando training had something to do with that. Camberley's was the brisk, firm step of the more orthodox soldier, but very little louder here. Sally was still wearing flat rubber-soled shoes and made almost no sound at all. Toby's caged leg dragged with a slow, soft scuffing; it was very tired at the end of a long day. The squeaking of the glass door as he opened it was strident in the quiet building.

The lights at this end of Peex were on; the far end lay in shadow. The men stood back to let Sally go in. So it was she who first rounded the end of the line of filing cabinets and saw Morningside. He was lying sprawled on his stomach just outside the open doorway of his office, with his head and shoulders out of sight inside it.

'He's ill,' she said, and went quickly forward.

Camberley said suddenly, 'Mrs Heldar—' and Johnny said, 'Sally, wait a minute,' but by that time she had almost reached Morningside.

Perhaps she had been dimly aware of the unnatural position which meant more to the two men who had been soldiers. Or perhaps their words and their tone had half prepared her. At any rate she wasn't taken totally by surprise. But when she stood by Morningside and looked down at his head — or what had been his head — with the black shower of shattered glass over and about it, she knew she couldn't stand it for long. She put out a hand to find the jamb, and Johnny's arm came round her.

'All right, darling,' he said. 'This way.'

He took her into Toby's office, turned on the light, put her into the chair at the desk, and looked rather anxiously at her. She saw that he was very pale himself.

'Don't worry,' she said. 'I'm not going to faint. Go and investigate.'

'Very well. I'll be just outside if you want me.'

Her head had steadied, but for a minute or two she wasn't at all sure she wasn't going to be sick. She concentrated on the voices beyond the half-open door of the room.

Camberley said quietly, 'We don't touch anything, of course. But this is your job, Heldar.'

'I'm no more qualified than anyone else, sir,' said Johnny. 'Will you ring up the police? Scotland Yard, I think. That's the first thing to do. They'll lay on a doctor quicker than we can, for what it's worth.'

'There's always an outside line plugged in to my telephone,' said Toby. His voice was under control, but not quite as even as Johnny's and Camberley's.

'It's a separate switchboard, isn't it?' asked Camberley. 'Good. We don't want an invasion of eager young men from the *Echo*. We must try to keep this as much to ourselves as possible. I know a man at Scotland Yard. If he's there he'll do his best for us.' He paused, and Johnny evidently answered some look or gesture from him.

'I think it must have fallen from the top of the door. It would make a hell of a row, of course, but presumably there was no one on this floor to hear it. I don't know about the next one below.'

Toby said dully, 'The floors are soundproof.'

Sally remembered the shattered negatives, the stout wooden box, still disgorging them, lying upside down almost on top of the shattered head, the single negative gripped in the groping fingers. For a moment she struggled again with nausea. She heard Camberley say almost in a whisper, 'Good God. A booby-trap.'

Then he came into Toby's office. His ruddy complexion was a little patchy. Toby, appearing in the doorway, was as white as a sheet. He said abruptly, 'There you are, sir. Will you excuse me a minute? I think I know where to find some whisky.'

'That's an excellent idea, Lorn.'

Toby scuffed away. Camberley looked at Sally with a steady reassurance, which was not quite a smile, and pulled another chair up to the desk. Sally pushed the telephone over to him, and he thanked her and dialled. Someone answered, and he said, 'Brigadier Camberley speaking. Is Superintendent Wigram by any chance still there?...Good. Thank you.'

There was a pause. Then he said, 'Hullo, Wigram. Listen. I'm speaking from the National Press Archives, which are on the top floor of the *Echo* building in Fleet Street. We've got a' — he hesitated, and then went firmly on — 'a fatality here...No, I don't think I can be much more specific. I honestly don't know what you'd call it, but perhaps it's nearer murder than anything else...A man called Frank Morningside — an Archives assistant...Thanks very much. I'm sorry you can't do it yourself, but I quite understand. Look here, Wigram. You know what Fleet Street is. Could your chaps arrive with as little publicity as possible? In fact, if they were to come up the alley on the east side of the building — it's called Thrale Passage — they'd find a side door... Fine. I'll tell the porter to expect them and show them the nearest lift, and there'll be someone at the top to bring them in...In about ten minutes? Thank you, Wigram. I'm very grateful. Goodbye.'

He rang off, looked kindly again at Sally, and asked, 'Better, Mrs Heldar?'

'Quite all right, thank you.'

'Well done,' he said, not casually but with emphasis. Then he rose, went to the door, and spoke to her and Johnny together.

'I talked to Superintendent Wigram — the man I know. He can't come himself; he's tied up at Scotland Yard, and anyway I don't think Superintendents go into action much these days. But he's sending us a chap called Lindesay — a Chief Detective-Inspector — who is evidently a very good man.'

Toby's scuffing step came back. He reappeared beside Camberley with a flask in his hand.

'Sorry to be so long. I had a bit of a job finding it,' he said.

He came over to Sally. She smelt no whisky and realised that he hadn't stopped to have a drink himself. He unscrewed the silver top of the flask, wiped it with a clean handkerchief, filled it with a slightly unsteady hand, and gave it to her. She didn't like whisky, but she knew she needed it. She drank it, not too fast. She didn't ask where it had come from; she knew that too. Michael Knox might easily be casual enough not to keep it locked up. He had been drinking this afternoon, she thought; not drunk, but having drink taken.

When she had finished Toby gave a tot to Camberley, and then they went out of sight beyond the door. She heard Johnny say, 'After you, Toby.'

Camberley came back into Toby's office, got on to the porter at the side door by way of the *Echo* switchboard, and said, 'Brigadier Camberley speaking, Laxton. The police will be coming in your way in a few minutes, to deal with a spot of trouble upstairs. Show them the back lift, and keep it quiet, will you? We'd like a bit of peace till we get sorted out.'

His voice was a mixture of authority and friendliness. Sally knew this gift for dealing with men; Johnny had it, but not quite to the same degree as Camberley, who had risen from the ranks to become a brigadier at thirty-eight and was said to have earned and retained the personal devotion of every man in his brigade.

He went back to Johnny and Toby, and Toby's voice said, 'This — this bloody thing must have been fixed up while we were in the canteen.'

'When were you in the canteen, exactly?' asked Johnny.

'We got there about a quarter to seven — that's when they start serving supper. The Brigadier had a date with Morningside, and when I said I was coming back here he asked me to join them. Morningside was there when we arrived; he's — he was always very punctual. But I shouldn't think he'd been there long; he was worried about leaving his office. And he left us about a quarter past seven, didn't he, sir?'

'I think so,' said Camberley. 'And we sat over our coffee for a few minutes longer.'

'Yes. He would have got here about twenty past — a little before.'

'And he'd have left here on his way to the canteen about twenty to — possibly earlier. Plenty of time to rig this thing, assuming the box of tricks was here. I believe it was — I believe I saw it when I was in his office this afternoon.'

'Yes,' said Toby. 'He was going to work on the negs this evening.'

Teddy had helped to bring the box up, thought Sally. Michael Knox had been in Morningside's office after that and might have noticed it. Toby had known it was there — but Toby, thank God, had an alibi. But the joker hadn't necessarily known it was there, just as on previous occasions he hadn't necessarily known there would be pictures to tear up or negatives to smash; it was quite likely he had come simply to see what damage he could find to do. He hadn't necessarily known that Morningside would be in the canteen, either. He must surely have known that Morningside was coming back to the office this evening, but the presence of an overcoat would make that clear. He might simply have rigged his trap on the spur of the moment. But he must have realised that it might easily kill Morningside. There could be no doubt now that he was insane.

Toby said suddenly, 'How did this — this joker get out when he'd rigged his trap?' Then he answered himself, 'Of course. By the hatch into my office. It's just about big enough.'

He moved towards his door, but Johnny said, 'Don't touch, Toby. Leave it for the police.'

Toby desisted and volunteered to go and receive the Inspector at the lift. He scuffed off again, and Johnny and Camberley came into his office. Camberley took the second chair again, and Johnny sat on the corner of the desk beside Sally. They were still sitting there when footsteps and voices sounded from the far end of the big room. They got up again, leaving her, and went out to meet the police.

Chief Detective-Inspector Lindesay had a pleasant voice which Sally identified as Lowland Scots. He asked them all to wait in the typists' office and was outside with his assistants for a while. Low voices and quiet movements came unintelligibly through the closed door. Johnny sat beside Sally, very steady, but with a grim white face. Camberley was like a rock, and Toby read the Post Office Directory with great assiduity.

Presently Inspector Lindesay looked in and asked the Brigadier if he might have a word with him. They went, apparently, into Toby's office. After about twenty minutes another plain-clothes man came to fetch Toby, but Camberley didn't come back. Obviously, no one who had been interrogated was to be given a chance of talking to those who were still waiting, even if he were a man of the Brigadier's standing. When Toby had gone Johnny pulled his chair closer to Sally's and tucked her hand under his arm. She had a strange feeling that he was asking for comfort as well as offering it, and she moved closer to him.

Nearly half an hour passed before he was sent for, and Sally spent nearly another half-hour alone. She studied the Post Office Directory carefully and at some length. By the time the second plain-clothes man came to fetch her she had read the names of all her neighbours in St Cross Square, all Old Father William Heldar's in Liphook Road, Wimbledon, all Uncle Charles's in Queen's Gate Row, and a good many other people.

Inspector Lindesay rose from behind Toby's desk as she came in. He was a Scot of the tall, lean, sandy-haired type whose age is always hard to judge; he might have been anything between thirty-five and fifty. His thin, high-boned, leathery face was a little austere.

'Come away, Mrs Heldar,' he said. 'I'm very sorry to have kept you so long. I'm afraid you'll be tired.'

'I'm quite all right,' said Sally, and sat down on the chair in front of the desk. 'Please tell me how I can help.' She was aware that the man who had fetched her had sat down behind her, no doubt to take notes, but that didn't worry her.

Lindesay looked at her with thoughtful frosty-blue eyes.

'I understand,' he said, 'that Mr Heldar has been en-quiring into this persecution of Mr Frank Morning-side. I think I've got the early history of it clear enough, but I'm interested in what you observed this afternoon and yesterday afternoon, while you were out there in the big room. Will you just tell me all the things that happened in your own words?'

She told him. She knew the list of yesterday's lunch-hour visitors by heart now. After what she had seen tonight, she had no scruples left. All but one of the people she was involving were presumably innocent, but if she wanted this madman caught, she had got to talk freely. She took her story right up to six o'clock this evening, when she had left Echo House with Toby and Camberley and Silcutt.

'And then you went home to St Cross Square,' said Lindesay, 'and you and Mr Heldar had supper? Now I understand Mr Lorn 'phoned Mr Heldar before you came back here. What time would that be, do you think? The 'phone call, I mean.'

'It was just after half past seven. We'd just finished supper, and I looked at my watch and asked my hus-band if we had time to wash up.'

'And how long was Mr Heldar on the phone, would you say?'

'Quite a little while. Perhaps four or five minutes. I'd done the washing and was getting ready to dry when he came in again.'

'I see. Now I'm very sorry, Mrs Heldar, but I want you to tell me about your discovery of Mr Morning-side's body. This doesn't mean I haven't asked Mr Heldar and Brigadier Camberley and Mr Lorn, but I want everybody's picture of it, you see. Will you take it from the moment you arrived back at Echo House?'

Probably he had taken the rest of her statement first to give her time to talk herself over the shock a little. Her evidence might be more reliable now. She did her best.

When she had finished, he nodded and said, 'Thank you, Mrs Heldar. I think that's all I need trouble you with tonight. You'll want to get away home. Kent, go and tell Mr Heldar that Mrs Heldar's ready to leave.'

They all went. Camberley and Toby were still here; they had evidently been sitting with Johnny in the typists' office. Downstairs in the hall Camberley asked the porter to get them two taxis, and they waited on the pseudo-Edwardian seat while he telephoned. The contemporary clock said twenty-five to eleven.

When the taxis came and they went out, Sally realised that it was raining hard now. Between the street lamps the pavement was black and shining like a black slug. The lamps sank broken reflections into it. The rain fell heavily on Sally's shoulders for a moment. Then Johnny put her into one of the taxis and followed her in. Camberley was going to take the other and drop Toby. In the dry, enclosed darkness, which smelt of cigarette smoke, Johnny put his arm round Sally and held her.

It wasn't very far. Presently they let themselves into the house and climbed the little curved staircase to the first floor. They crossed the narrow landing and went into the drawing room. The fire hadn't been lit and it was very cold.

Sally turned to Johnny and said, 'Darling, you mustn't look like that. Please.'

He didn't answer for a moment. Then he said very quietly, 'This is my fault, you know, Sally. Lindesay said we ought to have come to the police, and he was plumb

right. If I'd insisted and not tried to sort it out myself,
Morningside would probably be alive now.'

'Don't talk nonsense,' said Sally. 'No one could have
known there was a really dangerous lunatic about.
Practical jokes don't usually turn fatal. The police
couldn't have foreseen it any more than you.'

'I don't know. They have far more experience of this
sort of thing. Anyway, the merest suggestion of the police might have made the joker let up on his tricks, if
only temporarily.'

Sally put her arms round him. 'It's no use torturing
yourself,' she said. 'I think you're wrong — I don't think
the police could have prevented it — I don't think a lunatic would have let up for the police or anyone else.
But don't go on brooding about it. Get down to it and
find the man.'

'The police will do that now.'

'There's no reason why you shouldn't work on it
too.' She knew he would go on torturing himself unless
he did.

'Well, we'll see,' he said. He smiled faintly at her, and
then took her hand and held it for a moment against his
lips.

* * *

BUT NEITHER OF them slept much that night. Towards
three in the morning they stopped trying not to disturb
each other and, moving quietly because of Nanny and
the children, went down to the kitchen and made tea. It
was warm there because of the stove which heated the
water. Johnny looked miserable, and Sally thought it
better to encourage him to talk about the case. He sat
with his elbows on the kitchen table and talked in a
quiet, worried voice.

'I asked Toby about the times at which the different

things happened, and he's not altogether clear about it. Most of the filthy letters were delivered by night, and a few by day. The poltergeist stuff also happened both by day and by night; he thinks it was fairly equally divided between the two but can't be quite sure. The real trouble is that he can't say that only the prep school stuff or only the ruder rhymes happened at night. He knows some of the ruder rhymes did, but he's not sure that some of the prep school stuff didn't. He thinks it unlikely that Silcutt will be any more definite. So — assuming it was our joker who killed Morningside, and that seems likely — the case is still wide open. There's Teddy — a deprived adolescent with a bad record, who was responsible for at least part of the Morningside persecution. And do you remember, incidentally, the night-porter who walked into a fire bucket after he'd reported Teddy's bonfire? There was a quality in that which the perpetrator probably saw as poetic justice. There's rather the same quality in a booby-trap rigged with a box of negatives which had made Morningside lose his temper with Teddy. And then there's Michael Knox, who is probably unhampered by a conscience, has some sort of record of violence, and had been drinking yesterday afternoon, when he had a quite serious quarrel with Morningside. He seems to be in love with Selina, and, justifiably or not, to have been jealous of Morningside. There's also a history of friction over pictures for his book. Then we have Selina herself, who was engaged to Morningside, and was on at least irritable terms with him the day before his death. We don't know how bad the terms were, or why; there's a lot that needs explaining there.'

'But, Johnny, she couldn't conceivably have lifted that box of negatives to the top of the door.'

'She couldn't have lifted it full. Given time, she could have emptied it and balanced it on the top of the

door and against the lintel — as it probably was balanced — and then filled it again. We ought to note that,
although she was mentioned in some of the letters, that
doesn't necessarily let her out. She might have mentioned herself to avert suspicion. Toby is out of it,
thank God, because he was in the canteen when the
trap must have been rigged. But there's Miss Quimper,
a highly emotional middle-aged spinster, perhaps
rather unbalanced. She evidently suffered acutely from
professional jealousy of Morningside, and she was very
worked up about him on Tuesday afternoon. Toby told
us, incidentally, that she was astonishingly muscular for
her size and had been moving these boxes about for
over thirty years. I don't suppose for a moment that she
could have lifted a full one to the top of the door, but
she could probably have rigged the trap quite quickly
by the emptying and refilling process, because she's accustomed to handling the negs and the boxes. Those are
all our suspects, I think.'

'Except Silcutt,' said Sally.

'Silcutt,' said Johnny almost irritably. 'Yes, if you
want him. But I can't see that he had any motive. Some
of these people probably have alibis, so we may be able
to bring it down a bit further. I'll ask Toby to try to find
out about that.'

Sally looked at him, and he nodded. 'Yes. You were
perfectly right, darling. I've got to keep on with this —
as far as I can without annoying the police, anyway. I'm
indirectly responsible for Morningside's death, so it's
up to me to find this joker if I possibly can.'

CHAPTER FIVE

The Press went to town over Morningside's death. It was fairly clear that, as Toby had said, the Archives were not much liked, and that any rules there might be about dog not eating dog were not considered to apply here. Fleet Street had discovered a great deal and made up the rest, and the newspapers were full of fantastic and macabre stories. Johnny brought an armful of them home at lunchtime, in the hope of finding something which would help him, and Sally read them conscientiously too, but got no good of them.

Toby came to St. Cross Square at six o'clock. The police had spent part of the day in the Archives, looking for alibis as well as for other things, and he had been able to persuade most of his colleagues to tell him what they had been doing on the previous evening.

Sally had the impression that he had found Selina a little difficult to deal with, but on her own statement she had left Echo House just after six and gone straight home by bus to her flat in Chelsea, which she had reached just after half past. Unfortunately the girl with whom she shared it hadn't come in till eleven, and she had no alibi. Unfortunately also she had been the last person, except Morningside, to leave the top floor of Echo House, and no one could bear witness to her departure, except perhaps the night-porter at the main entrance, whom Toby hadn't seen. Even if she were vouched for at that point, no one could say for certain that she hadn't come back. Since the bonfire on Guy Fawkes night, the night-porter at the side entrance had been in the habit of making a brief round of Garrick Square, Thrale Passage, and two or three neighbouring alleys between half past six and a quarter to seven, after all the day-staff had gone home. This took him a matter of five minutes: not long, but quite long enough to allow someone to enter unnoticed by the side door.

Miss Quimper had worked late. She had left the building, she said, a little after half past seven, and had gone straight home by bus to her bedsitting room in Gloucester Road, reaching it about eight o'clock. A female friend in the same boarding house had been with her from that time until about ten. But that, as Toby pointed out unhappily, was no help at all. During the crucial period — twenty to seven until twenty past — she had been, on her own statement, alone in the Negatives Department; the last of her assistants had left a little before six. She was in the habit of working late two or three times a week, but not generally till as late as seven-thirty.

Silcutt had left the building with Sally, Camberley, and Toby at about six o'clock. He said he had gone straight home to Putney by tube from the Temple. He was a bachelor, and it had been his housekeeper's evening off, so no one could support his statement that he had reached his house at about seven o'clock and remained there. He could have returned to the *Echo* building and slipped in by the side door while its porter was out on patrol, but no one could see why he should have wanted to. He had voluntarily provided Toby with an account of his movements after Toby, supported by Camberley, had persuaded him to let Johnny carry on with his investigation.

Teddy said he had left Echo House at five-thirty. This statement was supported by Bill and the two other messengers, and more credibly by the side-door day-porter. He had reached home at ten or five to six, and taken high tea with his aunt and uncle, who would presumably corroborate him here. He had left the house again at about six-fifteen and gone to the pictures — alone. He had wanted to get there at six-thirty, which was why he had hurried over his tea.

'And I'm quite certain that's a lie,' said Toby. 'Or at least there's a lie lurking somewhere in it. I could tell by the look in his eye. I asked him if he could describe the films, and he gave me a graphic account of a Western with Dick Ray. But it could have been any Western. And he couldn't remember much about the other. He said it was sentimental, and he went to sleep.'

'Did he say which cinema it was?' asked Johnny.

'The Alcazar in the King's Cross Road.'

Johnny made a long arm, picked up the A to D volume of the Telephone Directory, found the number he wanted, and dialled it. After a moment he said, 'Good evening. Would you mind telling me what your programme is tonight?...Thank you so much. And it was the same last night?...Thank you. Goodnight.'

'Yes,' he said, replacing the receiver. 'Dick Ray in *Injun Trail*, and Gillian Davis in *Mothers' Day*.'

'That's exactly what Teddy said.'

'The Alcazar is probably his local cinema. He'd know what was on, or he could very easily find out. So he could have been back at Echo House by the time the night-porter was looking round outside. What about Knox?'

'Mike,' said Toby with some exasperation, 'is not

talking. He said he left the Archives about a quarter to six, but he refused in so many words to tell me how he had spent his evening and said he had likewise refused to tell Lindesay. He added that if I liked to assume, he was protecting a woman's fair name I was at liberty to do so. From which I deduce that he isn't, but you never quite know with Mike. I'll ask round about in Fleet Street — he's a well-known figure, and I may get something.'

Toby sat back in his chair and sipped his drink. But he didn't relax, and after a little Johnny asked, 'Anything else biting you? Apart from the general situation, I mean.'

'Not really. We had a mild professional crisis today. Some pix went missing — the entire file on Venezuelan revolutions — and we haven't found them yet. Presumably someone's put them away in the wrong place; it's happened before. In the meantime the editor of a well-known magazine is clamouring for them.'

'When you say it's happened before, you mean it's been someone's mistake?'

Toby looked faintly surprised. 'We imagine so. We mislaid the stuff on the Hungarian Rising a few days ago. The file was apparently missing one day and back in its place a couple of days later. It's amazing what mistakes people can make, you know.'

'I do,' said Johnny abstractedly. He was silent for quite a minute, lighting a pipe with sure, unhurried fingers. Then he asked, 'You are quite sure the things weren't in their proper places all the time? People can slip up over that too.'

'I know. We all know, so in a case like that we always do a double or even a triple check. Morningside found the Hungarian stuff missing, I remember, and Selina and I checked that it was. The file itself had been taken out. And this afternoon one girl found the

Venezuelan stuff missing and another girl checked. Same thing — file gone. It was there at five-thirty yesterday evening, too. But even the first incident couldn't have been part of the persecution, Johnny. It was a most ordinary occupational irritation, and anyway no one could have known he was going to want the Hungarian stuff. *Thought* rang up and asked for it twenty seconds before he went to look for it.'

'I see. Tell me, do you have a corresponding negative in the basement for every photograph upstairs?'

'Yes — except in some cases where a neg happened to be lost or broken before the pic came to us. Even then we make a copy neg if it's important.'

'Just so. Then you'd have negs of the Hungarian and Venezuelan stuff?'

Toby sat up and his face changed. 'Yes,' he said. 'Yes, because that's quite recent and comes from properly organised agencies. It's only older negs and negs in private ownership that have been lost or damaged, as a rule. And it was some Hungarian negs that Miss Quimper missed. From the filed stuff. She missed them the day before Morningside was killed — no, the day before that: Monday. She didn't report it to me till Tuesday; she thought they might turn up. And the Hungarian pix were missing on Friday — and back in their place on Monday. You know, I thought it seemed odd that Morningside should have been messing about with the filed negs.'

'This is rather interesting,' said Johnny. 'Toby, have you got to give evidence at the inquest tomorrow morning? Yes, well, so have I, and Sally wants to be there. Would it be possible (a) for Selina or someone to watch the filing cabinet where the Venezuelan pix should be, and (b) for Miss Quimper to watch the box or whatever it is where the Venezuelan negs pr ably are?'

Toby nodded slowly. 'It's not easy to watch one particular point, especially for a Peex assistant, who has to
attend to clients, but I'll ask them to do their best. But
do you think this has got anything to do with Morningside's death?'

'Frankly, no. But I think it'll bear investigation,
Toby. And remember, if anyone goes to the file or the
box, he mustn't on any account be tackled. He — or she
— must be observed and allowed to go away again. I
don't think either the pix or the negs are in any danger,
you know.'

* * *

TOBY WAS PERSUADED to stay for supper, but he said he
had an article for *The New Conservative* which should
have been finished a week ago and left a little before
nine o'clock. Sally and Johnny listened to the news, in
case there was anything about Morningside's death.
There were the still hoped-for summit talks, a colliery
strike, a by-election somewhere, an IRA raid on an
Army camp on Salisbury Plain, and various other items.
But to the Heldars' relief there was nothing about
Morningside.

Johnny had just switched the wireless off when the
telephone rang. Sally, who was beside it, picked up the
receiver and gave their number.

'Good evening, Mrs Heldar,' said a deep voice with
the hint of a country accent. 'James Camberley speaking. I hope you're all right — over the worst of it now?'

'Thank you,' said Sally. 'Yes, I'm absolutely all right.'

'I'm glad to hear it. I don't want to sound patronis-
ing, but I hope you'll let me say that I was overcome
with admiration. I shouldn't have thought any woman
could take a thing like that without a grain of fuss,
short of being completely callous. You make the way of

the investigator very easy for your husband. Which brings me to the second object of this call. May I speak to him?'

'Of course, Sir James. Here he is.' She added with some embarrassment, 'I'm afraid you're too generous,' and held out the receiver to Johnny, who came and sat on the arm of her chair. She put her head close to his and listened.

'Good evening, sir,' he said.

'Good evening, Heldar. Lorn told me he was going to report to you this evening on alibis and so on, and I've found something which must be added to his report. I don't like it a bit — we've caught someone out in a lie, at the best — and I don't much like passing it on, but I've no choice. Miss Marvell evidently told the police she left Echo House just after six yesterday evening and went straight home. Well — she didn't go straight home. She left just after six; the night-porter at the Fleet Street entrance saw her go. But he saw her come back, about ten to seven, and go up in one of the lifts. He can't remember when she left again; he was out of the hall for a few minutes round about half past seven, and she may have gone then. I spoke to the only lift-man on duty, and he says he's almost sure he didn't take her up or down. As you know, there's no man on the second lift at night. Brown — that's the porter — says there were several people in the hall when she came back at ten to seven, so I suppose she may have thought she'd had cover enough to slip in unnoticed.'

'That's possible,' said Johnny. 'She may not realise that she's rather striking.'

'Possibly not, though I don't suppose it's for want of telling. Brown is fully aware of her charms; that's why he noticed her. I thought I'd have a chat with him about people's movements, and this came out.'

'I'm very grateful, sir. I take it he's told the police?'

'Oh, yes. Reluctantly, I gather. I imagine they've confronted her with his evidence, but I don't know.'

'Well, perhaps I'll talk to her presently,' said Johnny, without enthusiasm.

'That's up to you. It's quite likely, of course, that she went back for some entirely innocent reason, and was afraid to admit it. I hope that's it, anyway. Goodnight, Heldar.'

'Goodnight, sir, and thank you.' Johnny put down the receiver, and Sally looked at him anxiously.

'I hate this,' she said. 'It's going to hurt Toby so much — even if she's only been pinching pictures. Johnny, you asked him to get her to watch the Venezuelan filing cabinet tomorrow morning. Is that desirable now?'

'I think we'll leave it as it is,' said Johnny. 'It'll be quite interesting to see what happens. I said, "Selina or someone", anyway, so he may not put her on to it. But I think, if nothing's happened by lunchtime, you or I must take it on.'

Sally nodded. She looked at his rather strained face, and said, 'What about some tea? And then perhaps bed? I'm sleepy.'

He agreed, and she went down to the kitchen and put the kettle on. She had made the tea and was coming up the curved staircase when she noticed that the drawing room door was a little ajar. The next moment it opened, and a thick green Penguin book fell on the mat outside. Johnny came out and picked it up. She realised suddenly what he was doing.

'Sorry, darling,' he said. 'I was just experimenting.'

'I know. Do you want any help?'

He looked doubtfully at her for a moment, and then said, 'Just once or twice, if you will.'

'Of course.' She carried the tray into the drawing room, put it down, and turned back to him. He was moving a straight-backed chair to a position behind the door.

'You'll want this to stand on,' he said. 'You have the door a couple of inches open and balance the book like this.' He reached up and placed it with its lower edge along the top of the door and its upper resting against the lintel. 'See?'

'Yes.' She took it from him, and he edged out of the room and pulled the door almost to behind him. She climbed on to the chair and placed the book, got off again, removed the chair, and said, 'All right.'

She heard Johnny's footsteps approaching, firm and brisk. The door opened. He had pushed it at arm's length, his hand on the handle, and the book struck him on the right forearm and fell on the mat again. He picked it up and gave it back to her. 'May we have it again?' he asked.

She did it again. This time he was close to the door when he opened it, and the Penguin just missed his head. The third time he pushed at arm's length again, and again got it on the forearm, and the fourth time he came close and it shaved his right ear. The fifth time it got him square on the head and came out of its cover.

'I'll mend it,' he said, and put it on top of the book-shelves. 'I think that's enough for tonight. Thank you, darling.'

CHAPTER SIX

The inquest was a long-drawn-out affair, and rather painful to the lay witnesses at least, though presumably not to the keen-faced men who reported it or the tightly packed little crowd of people which their stories and headlines had brought to the Coroner's Court.

The Coroner sat with a jury. He called first the police surgeon who had examined Morningside's body, and then the pathologist who had done the post-mortem — no doubt because they were busy professional men whose time was precious. They were agreed that Morningside had died of a fracture of the skull — though they didn't put it as simply as that — which had undoubtedly been caused by the box of negatives falling from the top of his office door. Their evidence was crisp but a little nightmarish, and Sally thought she saw the faces of the reporters sharpen. The police surgeon was characteristically reluctant to commit himself very closely as to the time of death. But his to-ings and fro-ings, as Toby called them afterwards, seemed to boil down to a virtual certainty that, from his point of view, Morningside had died — probably almost instantaneously — between approximately seven and eight o'clock, or, roughly speaking, between an hour and an hour and a half before witness had first seen him. But the evidence of Camberley and Toby, which came later, put it beyond doubt that he had been alive until after a quarter past seven, and suggested strongly that he had died just about twenty minutes past.

Inspector Lindesay was called after the doctors and described his first visit to the National Press Archives and what he had done there. He was followed by a fat woman in black, who was Morningside's aunt and next of kin, and identified his body with a garrulity perhaps due to shock. The other lay witnesses came after her.

The Coroner treated Camberley with great respect, but Camberley gave it back again. He was a first-class witness, careful, accurate, and beautifully clear. The pens and pencils of the reporters recorded him eagerly, and Sally was rather sorry for him. He never seemed to seek publicity, although he accepted it in his own entirely unselfconscious fashion, and she was sure this kind was not to his simple but unerring taste. But it was a greater ordeal for Toby. He spoke quietly and calmly, and the only sign of strain was a certain whiteness about his mouth. Perhaps only the Heldars guessed at the effort he was making.

Johnny came last and was very unemphatic and very convincing. Since — as the Coroner pointed out to the jury in his summing-up — the proceedings and evidence at an inquest were directed solely to ascertaining who the deceased was, how, when and where he came by his death, and the persons, if any, to be charged with the crime, if the jury found that a crime had been committed, it was probably considered unnecessary as well as inexpedient to bring up the history of the persecution at this stage, and the Coroner required no particular reason for Johnny's presence at the discovery of the body.

The Coroner, having made clear the objects of the enquiry and summed up the evidence, explained to his jury that it was for them to decide on matters of fact. He was here only to guide them on matters of law. It was for them to decide how the box of negatives — the instrument of death — had got on to the top of the door. If they thought it, as they well might, extremely unlikely that the deceased had put it there himself and brought it upon his own head, the verdict of suicide was inappropriate. If they thought it equally unlikely that any form of carelessness, however blameworthy, had brought it there by accident, then the verdict of death by misadventure was equally inappropriate, and even a verdict of manslaughter was inadmissible. If, on the other hand, they believed that some other person had deliberately placed the box on the top of the door with the intention or in the hope of killing or injuring Francis Morningside, then — even if that person could not have been absolutely certain of causing Francis Morningside's death — it was their duty to bring in a verdict of murder. If they were satisfied that the evidence they had heard pointed to any particular person or persons, it was their duty to bring in a verdict of murder against that person or those persons. If, on the other hand, they were not so satisfied...

The jury, quite satisfied that the Coroner was right, consulted together in whispers and, without retiring, brought in a verdict of murder against some person or persons unknown.

The lay witnesses left the Court tightly packed in the crowd. Morningside's aunt was well ahead, skilfully piloted by an indeterminate male escort. Johnny kept Sally's arm in his, and Toby, who ought to have had a stick, moved with some difficulty on her other side. Camberley and Silcutt, who had been an obviously reluctant observer, were somewhere behind them.

'Oi! Lorn!' said a thin middle-aged man with a note-book. 'Got a story for an old friend?'

'No, I haven't, damn your eyes,' said Toby amiably. 'Put away your horrid little notebook and run back and turn in what you've got already. You won't get any more from me.' He had taken Sally's free arm and was edging her and Johnny unobtrusively away.

But it was too late. 'Good morning, Mr Heldar,' said another voice. 'You interesting yourself in this case?'

'Give me a chance,' said Johnny with a grin. 'If I'd stayed away, I'd have been arrested for contempt of court or whatever it is.'

A camera flashed. Toby's friend said, 'Funny thing you and Mrs Heldar should have found the body, though — don't you think? Come on, Mrs Heldar. Take pity on a poor newspaperman and tell me what your famous husband's after.'

Sally looked at her watch. 'I think his lunch,' she said gently. 'It's getting on for one o'clock.'

There was a general laugh, and then Camberley came up behind them and got them into a taxi. Sally was grateful to him; the exchange of badinage with the Press wasn't really her line.

He insisted on giving them lunch, and only Silcutt refused the invitation. He was obviously very shaken, more by the publicity of the proceedings than by any-thing else, and Camberley didn't press him. They dropped him and went on.

'Funny,' said Camberley thoughtfully. 'I've never got to the bottom of that man, and I don't suppose I ever shall. He seems so transparent, and then suddenly you realise you don't really know him at all.'

He took them to a surprisingly quiet pub in the City and ordered drinks. 'I don't usually drink at lunchtime,' he said, 'and perhaps you don't either. But I think we need it today.'

They had an excellent lunch and felt rather better for it. Camberley was known here, and their waiter was very attentive. The Brigadier refused to discuss the case while they ate, and it was only over coffee that he returned to it. He looked at Toby and said, 'Did you get anything from Laxton? I was going to have a chat with him myself, but I saw you using your reporter's wiles on him and I thought I'd leave him to you.'

Toby grinned, and then looked worried. 'Yes, I got something. I meant to go home and write, as I said' — he looked at Sally — 'but I changed my mind and went detecting instead. Laxton is the side-door night-porter, incidentally. When he came on duty last night, he had a talk with the side-door day-porter about our spot of trouble, and they compared notes about the police interrogation. The day man had been asked in the morning when the Archives messengers had left the building on the previous evening, and he'd said they'd all walked out on the stroke of five-thirty, as usual. That was a minute or two before Laxton came on. The boys always use the side door, and they're never a moment after five-thirty unless they're up to something. Now Laxton had been asked in the course of the previous night if anyone from the Archives had gone out or come in while he was on duty, and he'd said yes, Teddy had gone out a little before seven o'clock. That was very late indeed for a messenger, and Laxton was extremely suspicious. He didn't challenge Teddy — he knew he'd only be checked — but he made sure the boy had really gone and then went and had another look at the messengers' room. I think I told you he's in the habit of looking round it when he first comes on duty. He'd found it normal on his first visit — and Teddy hadn't been there — and he found it normal again.

'Well, he and the day man deduced that Teddy had probably slipped in while he was doing his round outside — which as far as he can remember was approximately between twenty-five and twenty to seven. I saw the night-porter at the Fleet Street entrance — one Brown — and he's pretty sure Teddy didn't come in his way. Lindesay, of course, must realise the implications, and he may have confronted Teddy with Laxton's evidence. But Teddy still lied to me about it.'

'Possibly,' said Johnny, 'he values your good opinion. Tell me this, Toby. In the absence of a porter's evidence to the contrary — and apart from moments when a porter was absent from his post — can we be sure that any given person didn't re-enter the building?'

'No,' said Toby slowly. 'The van entrance in Garrick Square is closed at that time, but Laxton says he has known the boys get in by some way of their own. He reckons it involves a coal-flap in the square and an inside door left open in advance. He doesn't know Teddy didn't get in that way on Wednesday evening, but judging by the time Teddy says he left home, his arrival probably coincided with Laxton's patrol outside. And he probably knew about the patrol.'

'I see. Any more news?'

'Yes,' said Toby. He looked rather more worried now, and Sally thought: He's heard about Selina. But he went on, 'It's Miss Quimper. When Laxton is at his desk inside the door he can't see the back lift, which is down a flight of steps and round a corner in another passage. He can't see anyone in its immediate vicinity, either. But when he came in after his patrol that evening, he went down the steps and round the corner to leave his coat, and when he came out of the Gents' he saw Miss Quimper come out of the lift and make for Negs. She doesn't use his door — most of the Negs people don't. I think it's a question of caste. But he knows her by sight, because she works late fairly often. He said she was looking rather upset. He hasn't told the police this — they only asked him if he'd seen any of the Archives people entering or leaving the building, and he didn't think of it at the time. That's what he says, anyway. But it may simply have been old-fashioned chivalry.'

'The time he saw her,' said Johnny, 'would be just after twenty to seven?'

'Something after a quarter to, he says. He stayed in the Gents', it seems, to wash out two pairs of socks — he's living in rooms where there's next to no hot water.' Toby hesitated. 'As far as I can see, Johnny, she must have been up to Peex or Cuts. We have no offices on any other floor, and as far as I know she has no friends on any other.'

'No, I see. Assuming Morningside started for the canteen at twenty to seven, and she was waiting to slip into his office as soon as he left it, she'd have five or six minutes to rig the trap. Not very long.'

'I had a word with the evening shift in the canteen,' said Toby reluctantly. 'The girls say Morningside arrived about two minutes before we did — he waited at the end of the counter. That means he could have left Peex as early as — let's say six-thirty-eight. The canteen's in the basement, and if the lifts are slow in coming one can spend about five minutes in transit.'

'Seven or eight minutes,' said Johnny. 'She'd have to take the negs out of the box and put them back again when it was in place. But she handles the stuff every day. And she'd have no difficulty in getting through your hatch; she's very small, and apparently quite active. I'm afraid she could have done it.'

'I'm afraid so too,' said Camberley quietly. 'Though I don't find it easy to suspect Miss Quimper. But then I don't find it easy to suspect anyone. Damn it, it's *not* easy to suppose that someone you see every day,

someone with whom you have friendly professional relations, is a dangerous lunatic.'

They were all silent for a moment. Sally felt a little
shiver pass over her.

Johnny noticed it. He said he would like to go back
to the Archives with Toby and asked her if she wanted
to get home.

'No,' she said. 'I'll come with you. We're out in the
open now, aren't we?'

'We are,' said Johnny. 'I'm just wondering how
people are going to take us.'

* * *

CAMBERLEY DROPPED THEM, at Toby's particular request,
a little way short of Echo House, and they slipped in by
way of Thrale Passage and the side door. It seemed that
one or two of the *Echo*'s young men might be lying in
wait for news in the entrance hall, and that this was in
any case the quickest way to the Negatives Department.
As they went down a steep flight of steps Toby said, 'By
the way, don't worry too much about your reception.
Camberley's paved the way for you. I don't suppose
Miss Quimper will fall on your necks, but she won't be
too difficult.'

But Sally, remembering the emotion Miss Quimper
had shown in Morningside's office, found the meeting
extremely embarrassing. Toby made introductions and
slipped away, leaving them to face the ugly, unhappy
woman they had spied on.

Miss Quimper took immediate refuge in an over-
brisk professionalism. 'Well, Mr Heldar?' she said. 'I
shall of course be glad to answer any questions you care
to ask me.'

'Thank you so much,' said Johnny. 'But won't you sit
down? We'll bring up these chairs, if we may.'

They were in a corner of the big basement room, which reminded Sally a little of Heldar Brothers' bookrooms. There were steel cases across its length, with low shelves rising in tiers almost to the low ceiling, and full of cardboard boxes, each carefully labelled and presumably containing negatives. Narrow alleys ran between the cases. Someone might be within two feet of you and you wouldn't know it. Someone might be within ten feet of Miss Quimper's desk now, listening, though there was no one to be seen.

Johnny said quietly, 'I think Mr Lorn asked you to try to keep an eye on the Venezuelan negatives, Miss Quimper. Have you managed to do that?'

'Yes, Mr Heldar. It was quite easy, because the negatives are at this end of the room, in the second gangway. I had only to move my chair a little to the right and I could see along it. It was really a little too easy, because anyone who was interested in the negatives would know that I could keep them under observation. So at lunchtime I didn't go to the canteen. I went and sat at the end of a gangway at the other end of the room, where I could see the door and the end of the second gangway.'

'I'm sorry you missed your lunch,' said Johnny. 'It was very good of you to give it up. Did anyone come?'

'No, Mr Heldar, I'm afraid not. And I checked ten minutes ago, and the negatives are still there. But I was going to suggest that you or Mrs Heldar should watch from the other end now, and I should go up to Pictures for a bit. Of course, if one of my own assistants is doing this, she may see you and be warned. But if it's someone from another department they won't wander round the shelving.'

Johnny considered for a moment. 'I think I'll do it,' he said. 'I want to go upstairs for a minute first, and I'll leave my wife there. But before we go, Miss Quimper,

I've got another question to ask you. I hope you'll forgive me, and not think it an impertinence. Why did you go up to Peex the evening before last?'

Miss Quimper didn't answer, but her face gave her away at once, and her big hands, folded on the desk in front of her, clasped each other convulsively.

Johnny waited, and at last she asked, 'How do you know?'

'Someone saw you come down after a quarter to seven.'

'Oh, yes. It was Laxton — the night-porter — wasn't it? I did see him. I hoped afterwards he'd forget.' Her harsh voice was shaking now; she sounded excited and a little hysterical.

'Why did you go up?' asked Johnny very steadily.

'I wanted to see Mr Morningside about my negs. I thought he'd been down here interfering with them and getting them into the wrong order. I thought he would be working late — he nearly always did on Wednesdays — so I went up and he was there.'

'What time was that, Miss Quimper?'

'About twenty-five to seven. I talked to him for about five minutes — no, perhaps not quite as much as that — and then he said he had to meet Brigadier Camberley in the canteen, and he went off to the lift — the main lifts. So I came down again.'

Johnny's manner had calmed her a little. But she was still frightened and tense.

'These negs, Miss Quimper. They were some of the old ones that the Archives have taken over, weren't they?'

'Yes. They'd obviously been handled — the dust on the bags had been disturbed — and I couldn't be sure they hadn't been disarranged. But there were some that were already in the files, too; they were actually missing, though on Wednesday afternoon I found they'd been put back.'

'Those were the negs of the Hungarian Rising, weren't they?'

'Yes,' she said, a little surprised. 'Anyhow, you see, I'd told Mr Lorn all about this on Tuesday afternoon. He said he'd speak to Mr Morningside about it, but on Wednesday afternoon I found that some more of the old negs had been handled, so I thought he couldn't have done it, and I decided I'd have to see Mr Morningside myself.'

'And what did Mr Morningside say?'

'He said he hadn't touched the Hungarian negs, and I thought at the time that might be true, because he'd have no particular reason for wanting them. Besides, he was an honest man; I don't think he'd have lied to me. And now you're looking for someone who may be interested in the negs of the Venezuelan Revolution, so I think he probably was telling the truth.'

Miss Quimper's voice was still a little unsteady. But a sudden shrewd intelligence was showing behind her pince-nez.

'And the old negs?' asked Johnny.

'Oh, he more or less admitted handling them. He said he had worries just now — he meant the jokes that were being played on him, obviously — and he was so upset he really didn't know what he was doing. Poor man,' said Miss Quimper, and her eyes filled with tears. 'I wish now I hadn't upset him. I can't forgive myself.'

Johnny said quietly — and Sally was very much aware of his reluctance, 'Did you quarrel with him before he went downstairs, Miss Quimper?'

'I don't know if you'd call it a quarrel or not. We had an argument. We were both very upset.' Her mouth was trembling. Sally saw a disquieting picture: the over-emotional middle-aged woman and the nerve-racked young man, facing each other in the little office, both of them wrought up to a pitch quite unwarranted by the subject of their argument, both very near the limit of self-control — or one of them, perhaps, passing beyond it.

Johnny went doggedly on. 'You said you went upstairs about twenty-five to seven, and talked to him for about five minutes, or possibly less. That would mean that you left him about twenty to seven, or perhaps a little before.'

'I think so, yes.'

'But Laxton saw you come out of the lift after a quarter to. It wouldn't take you all that time to get down that way, would it?'

'No,' she said. 'I went into the Ladies' Cloakroom between Pix and Cuts. I — I wanted to wash my face.'

They left her after that. Johnny looked savage, and Sally knew it was with himself. She slipped her arm into his, and they found the back lift, which had no operator. As they went up, he pulled himself together and said, 'If no one's restored the Venezuelan pix you can watch the file, for what it's worth. All the staff know we're investigating Morningside's death; we can only hope they don't all know we're interested in the missing pix.'

The lift landed them in a short corridor. Sally saw glass doors with a notice beside them which said 'Press Cuttings', the stairhead, the Ladies' and Gents', and the glass doors which led into Peex. They went that way, and Johnny knocked on the door of Toby's office. Toby's voice called, 'Come in.'

He got up when he saw Sally. 'Come and sit down,' he said, and added when Johnny had shut the door, 'I'm sorry to have to tell you that Selina saw no one approach the Venezuelan file. It was too difficult — she couldn't keep her eye on it all the time, and she didn't like to enlist anyone else, because for all she knew one of our own assistants was the guilty party. She didn't go to lunch — she stayed here and did what she could. But when I got back after lunch the pix had been replaced.'

'Damn,' said Johnny philosophically. 'Never mind. In that case I'm going straight down again to watch the negs. Sally, if you want to go home, do.'

'You wouldn't like me to do the negs?' asked Sally. 'Then you could get on with whatever you want to do here.' But she knew he wouldn't let her go alone to that place of mysterious, dusty alleyways. Up here there were light and space and clients to make for safety, and Toby to look after her. Down there it would be too easy to strike a blow in the shadows. She reminded herself that no one was at all likely to want to strike a blow at her. Johnny knew that too. But he wouldn't be quite rational about it either.

'I haven't got anything I want to do here,' he said.

'Then let me come with you. You'd be just as suspicious by yourself as we shall be together, if anyone noticed you.'

'Very well,' he said after a moment. 'Toby, would you mind ringing down to Miss Quimper and asking her to come up here? She was kind enough to say she'd leave us a clear field.'

'Right,' said Toby. 'Oh, by the way, I forgot to tell you that I spent an hour or so in public 'ouses last night, round about here, and I found one man who was talking to Michael Knox on Wednesday evening. It was in the Cat-in-Boots — not very far from Echo House — somewhere between six and half past. The barmaid thinks Mike was there a bit later than that, but she can't be sure. Incidentally, I hear he hasn't been seen about Fleet Street nearly so much in the last month or so. Of course he's been here most of the day and most people assume he's working on his book in the evenings. But I'm not so sure it's just that. Mike likes his drink, but that's not really the point. The point is that Fleet Street is meat *and* drink to him, and I can't see him keeping off it for long for the sake of any book.'

'That's interesting,' said Johnny. 'You might keep on asking about his movements on Wednesday evening, Toby.'

They left Toby's office, and in the back passage ran into Knox himself.

'Good afternoon to you,' he said, and his dark face was amused and cynical at the same time. 'You've made a proper fool of me, the pair of you. At my time of life I should know a detective when I see one. I should have recognised you from Press photographs, too. And the best I can do is to talk politics and association football to one of you and pay insipid compliments to the other.'

Sally looked into his amused eyes and was stung to retaliation.

'You mustn't worry,' she said kindly. 'You only want a little more practice.'

She got home, but the amusement was back in a second.

'Thank you, Mrs Heldar,' said Knox meekly. 'I hope you'll be kind enough to help me. Well, now, what can I do for you both? I'm sure there are questions you would like to ask me.'

Johnny thought for a moment. 'No, I don't think so,' he said placidly. 'Thank you all the same.'

It was more successful than Sally's effort. Knox's black eyebrows rose very slightly. 'No? All right. Good luck to you, then.'

When they were in the lift Johnny laughed almost wholeheartedly for the first time in two days.

'He had you there, my love.'

'I should have known better than to take him on. You did rather well, darling.'

'I will not let that man take a rise out of me. I know damn well he won't tell me where he was when Morningside was killed, and it isn't the slightest use asking him. We shall just have to find out some other way.'

They found Miss Quimper waiting for the lift in the basement passage. She nodded briefly to them and stepped in, and they went on to Negs. They turned left inside the glass doors and went along to the last gangway. Someone — presumably Miss Quimper herself — had left a chair at this end of it, and Johnny pushed Sally gently down.

The place was nearly dark. The nearest fluorescent bar was a little way off. The shadows were thicker at the far end of the gangway, and presently Sally realised that it was closed, or almost closed, by a case standing at right angles to it.

Time passed slowly. Footsteps and voices sounded muffled; it was difficult to judge their distance. Johnny and Sally, sharing the chair, saw Miss Quimper's girls moving now and then between the gangways. But none of them came into the last gangway, and no one else appeared.

The Heldars had come in just before half past three. Towards four o'clock the girls began to drift out; one of them said clearly, 'Well, I'm going to have tea before she comes back and gives me something more to do.' Probably they were supposed to go to the canteen in equal shifts. But a little after the hour three out of the four of them had slipped away.

Sally was stiff and a little cold, though she and Johnny were still wearing their coats. Watching had become a mechanical thing, and when Teddy sidled into the room and round to the right it took her a moment or two to grasp the possible significance of what was happening. She woke up to it when he turned into the second gangway and Johnny's arm, which was round her shoulders, tightened suddenly.

But he made no other movement. He waited, and after two or three minutes Teddy reappeared, with his right hand in the pocket of his long black jacket. Walking very fast, and looking very pale, he passed out through the glass doors and disappeared.

Johnny got swiftly to his feet, lifting Sally to hers. 'Go up to Toby,' he said quietly, 'and tell him I think Teddy is responsible for the missing negs and pix. No action is to be taken, please, and no one else is to know yet. I'm going to make sure — Teddy may be sent out any minute, and he may take advantage of it. When you've seen Toby, go home. I mean that. You are not to come back here, and you are not to linger too long upstairs. Understand?'

Sally understood. Johnny seldom gave her orders, but when he did, she had no choice. If she disobeyed him, she would be left out of it next time.

'Yes,' she said. 'Promise.'

They left Negs. Raucous adolescent voices coming from beyond an open door at the far end of the passage indicated the messengers' room. Johnny left Sally outside the lift and started off towards the front of the building.

She had reached Peex and was approaching Toby's door when one of his assistants, coming up from another direction, saw her and stopped short.

'I'm so sorry, Mrs Heldar,' she said. 'After you.'

'I'm in no particular hurry,' said Sally. 'If you want to see Mr Lorn—'

'I just want some pictures from his office. There's no hurry for me either. Please go on, Mrs Heldar.'

Sally smiled and thanked her, knocked on the door, thought she heard Toby's voice, and walked in. The office was empty. She hesitated, puzzled, and then she heard Toby's voice again. It was coming from beyond the glass hatch, which was an inch or two open, and it was very quiet and steady.

'You know if there's anything I can do to help I shall be very glad to do it.'

'You're being extremely fatherly.' It was Selina's voice, and curiously taut. 'You want me to confess to you again?'

'No, I don't. I'm not asking you to talk about it if you don't want to. You know I have no feelings about what you did to Morningside that evening. He'd done a good deal to you. I should only like to help you as much as I can if you're unhappy — if you want to sort yourself out at all. Would you like to have dinner somewhere tonight?'

Sally had made a move to leave Toby's office. Then she had seen the assistant hovering. Anything was better than that one of Toby's own staff should overhear this. She shut the door loudly. But Toby and Selina either didn't hear it or didn't realise how audible they were themselves. Sally stood still, looking out of the big window and down over the low parapet outside to the bombed site below.

'That's big of you,' said Selina. 'You sound like Frank. I ought to lead a godly, righteous, and sober life, and if I do, you'll consent to be seen about with me. Thank you. But if I dine with anyone I'll dine with Mike. At least he doesn't invest the evening with an odour of sanctity. Or I might even get Lionel Silcutt to take me out. He can't dance, but he's much more of a ladies' man than you'd think.'

The door of Morningside's office opened. Sally heard quick, light footsteps pass Toby's, and took a chance. She walked straight out and was in time to see Selina sweep past an assistant, who tried to speak to her, and make for the glass doors at the Cuts end. There was no sign of Toby. Sally moved idly away. The assistant who wanted pictures went into his office and presently reappeared. Then he came out of Morningside's. He was very white and looked a little dazed. But he saw Sally and said, 'Hullo. Were you looking for me?' His voice and manner were peculiarly gentle.

He might protect Selina, but he would scarcely protect Teddy, and the story of the negs might prove a counter-irritant. Sally nodded, and he took her into his office.

'Teddy,' he said when she had finished. 'Yes, of course he may be sent out any time. I could keep him in, but I gather Johnny's all set.'

'I think so. I imagine he's lurking outside somewhere. Will you come to supper, Toby, and hear his news?'

'Sweet of you, Sally, but I've still got that article to do. I'll ring up later, if I may.'

Sally repressed the urge to say something warm and comforting and went away. She used the side door again, and might have gone through Garrick Square, but curiosity about Johnny took her back down Thrale Passage and into Fleet Street.

Someone was concealed behind a newspaper in the doorway of a small restaurant, closed at this hour, on the corner of the passage. As she passed the newspaper was lowered for a moment and Johnny winked at her. She winked back.

CHAPTER SEVEN

She got home in time to have the children in the drawing room for a while. They had had a rather thin time of it after tea for the last few days, and Peter at any rate had felt it. He was particularly uproarious this evening. The twins were easier to handle; Charles was observant rather than active, and Celia was a placid child. Nanny came for them at a quarter to six, and Sally managed to calm Peter down by reading to him.

He had already asked several times where Daddy was, and she was beginning to wonder herself. When Nanny had come back for him, she went down to the kitchen and did something towards supper. It was after half past six when she started upstairs to say goodnight. She had just reached the first-floor landing when the telephone rang. Johnny, she thought. Or possibly Toby. She ran into the drawing room and answered it there.

But it was a woman's voice which spoke — a familiar voice, harsh but a little unsteady.

'Is that Mrs Heldar? This is Miss Quimper speaking. I'm sorry to disturb you, but I wondered if I might speak to Mr Heldar.'

'I'm so sorry,' said Sally, 'but he's not in yet. Could I give him a message?'

Miss Quimper was silent for so long that Sally went on, 'Or would you rather he rang you up when he gets in?'

'No — I'll tell you, if I may.' Miss Quimper was growing more agitated. 'Your husband was so kind this afternoon — you both were. I think I can trust him.' She hesitated again, and then went straight into it.

'I told you this afternoon that I saw Mr Morningside in Pix about twenty-five to seven that evening. I told you what I said to him and he said to me.' (Sally was absurdly reminded of Consequences.) 'But some of it — a little of it — was said the second time. After I went down at a quarter to seven, I kept worrying about it, because I hadn't properly understood whether he was responsible for handling the old negs or not. So I gave him till nearly half past seven and then went up again. He'd said he was coming back after he'd had supper. I went up in the back lift again, and the light was on in Cuts. I looked in, and he was looking for something in one of the filing cabinets — he said Brigadier Camberley had asked him for a cutting and was in a hurry for it. He must have come up by one of the main lifts and straight through Pix — he obviously didn't — didn't — go into his own office first.'

'Obviously not,' said Sally gently. 'I'm so glad you've told us this, Miss Quimper.'

'I don't know if it'll help Mr Heldar. But it was on my conscience, and I felt it would be easier to tell him than the police. Anyhow, Mr Morningside was in a hurry — or he said he was. I think he was really so upset and nervy he couldn't stand being bothered. I stayed for a couple of minutes while he found his cutting, and then we both came out. He went back into Pix, and I went down in the lift again and then home.'

'I see,' said Sally. 'Thank you very much, Miss Quimper. And don't worry. I can't promise that my husband won't tell the police, but he'll sort things out. Are you at home, just in case he wants to ring you up?'

'I shall be home in about half an hour. I'm still in Fleet Street — I came up to Mr Lorn's office to phone. The switchboard is in Cuts, and the girls there always go off at five-thirty — Mr Knox is rather lax — and they don't leave a line plugged through to Negs.'

Poor Miss Quimper, thought Sally, writing down the telephone number of the boarding house. She mightn't have had to work late if they hadn't turned her out of her own department this afternoon. On a sudden impulse, Sally asked her if she wouldn't come to supper and see Johnny, but she refused. She had unloaded her conscience, and she was evidently tired. Sally was rather relieved; Johnny would probably be tired too. But she was very sorry for Miss Quimper. It came suddenly home to her that she might have spent her whole life as Miss Quimper was spending hers, living alone, working too long, exaggerating small irritations, taking any real trouble painfully hard, becoming a trial and an embarrassment to everyone who had to do with her. And instead of that she had Johnny, and the uproarious Peter and the fat twins upstairs in bed. She went on to say goodnight to them, feeling that she could never be sufficiently thankful.

Johnny appeared while she was still with Peter, in time to tell his usual Albert story. Albert was Peter's Teddy Bear, and the stories about him made a saga which would probably not end till the twins became too old for it. Johnny was infinitely ingenious and infinitely patient.

But when they were in the drawing room and she had given him a drink he started on a different story.

'As you know, I waited at the mouth of Thrale Passage. That doorway was a bit of luck, but I should have preferred to wait in Garrick Square, because the side door of Echo House is almost on the corner of it, and I knew I might lose Teddy if he went that way. But when I explored it, I found there was no cover at all, and it was quite empty of passersby, so I felt I couldn't risk it.

'I very nearly did lose Teddy when he came out — that was about half past four. He cut through the square and led me at a spanking pace through a succession of alleys and lanes between bombed sites. I was convinced he was going to look round any minute and I was going to look the most frightful fool. I haven't been trained to follow people. This went on for about four minutes, at the end of which he stopped outside an office building, handed an official packet to a large commissionaire, uttered some piece of rudeness, and turned and walked briskly back again — mercifully without noticing me. And that was that trip.

'I waited in my doorway again, feeling just like a private detective and quite sure I looked like one. I waited till nearly half past five, and then Knox came out by the front door and passed me. Unfortunately he recognised me. He started very slightly, but he pulled himself together at once and said, "Hullo! This is extremely interesting. The operative on the job. How are you getting on?" I was irritated, and I knew Teddy might appear any minute, so I told him to be a good chap and get to hell out of it; I wasn't interested in him. He grinned and went off, but I think,' said Johnny reflectively, 'he thought I was deliberately misleading him. When he'd gone about twenty yards he looked very quickly over his shoulder. I'm not quite sure which of us had the best of that encounter.

'I was just recovering from it when Teddy came out into Fleet Street. He didn't notice me; he went straight off in the direction of Ludgate Circus. The pavement was crowded, and he was in a hurry, and the only thing I was afraid of this time was losing him. At the Circus he turned into Farringdon Street. Beyond Farringdon Underground he turned right, into a narrow street called Farringdon Row. A little way up it he disappeared into a shop doorway. I passed by, cautiously, on the other side, and saw that he'd gone in. A blind was down over the door, so he'd evidently been let in after shop hours. But there were no blinds over the window. And the window display, Sally, was photographic equipment.'

'You mean he was taking his negatives to be printed?'

'I think so. By private arrangement, I fancy, with a buddy of his who is probably the shop assistant. I went back to the corner of Farringdon Street and waited behind my newspaper and walked up and down for about an hour. Then Teddy reappeared with a very flash type of twenty or thereabouts. I'd followed them about fifty yards when Teddy suddenly decided to run for a bus which was going back towards Ludgate Circus. I don't think he'd seen me, though. His friend picked up a girl, and I found a taxi and came home.'

'But,' said Sally, 'is he selling the prints?'

'I think he must be. I've been working it out. According to Toby, the Archives make no charge for letting people look at a picture, but they ask a minimum of thirty shillings apiece for any pictures which are reproduced. Teddy must obviously undercut their price, and I don't see that he can ask more than a guinea, even if he's only selling one or two pictures to his client. Out of that he most certainly gives a cut to his buddy — that young man has never done anything for nothing in his life. I should think he takes at least half a crown a print, depending on number and size. But fifteen shillings to eighteen and six, say, would be quite good going from Teddy's point of view. Not from everyone's, though. For instance, I didn't really think Selina was pinching pix. For someone with a higher-grade salary it almost certainly wouldn't be worth the risk. A typist was possible, but a messenger was more likely, and given Teddy's record he was the most likely of all.' Johnny paused to light another cigarette.

'One can see the sequence,' he said, 'both with the Hungarian Rising stuff and here. The Hungarian pix were missing last Friday and back in their place on Monday. The Hungarian negs were missing on Monday and back in their place on Wednesday afternoon. But in this case, we can go into more detail. The Venezuelan pix were in their place on Wednesday afternoon at five-thirty. Teddy came back a little after six-thirty and collected them — presumably he hadn't found an opportunity of so doing during working hours. Presumably, again, he showed them to his client either on Wednesday evening or sometime on Thursday — that is, yesterday — and his client made a selection and placed an order. He may have tried to return them yesterday, but the police were in the Archives for the better part of the day, and he's out a good deal. He succeeded in replacing them, unobserved, some time this morning, and this afternoon he took the corresponding negs. All pix have a number, and generally speaking, I gather, all negs have a corresponding number, so he wouldn't have to compare them; he would just have a scrap of paper with the numbers on it. This evening he had the prints made; his buddy could do a very good job in an hour, or indeed in less. What worries me is that he may have gone straight off after that to deliver them to his client. But we can only hope not. He'll probably replace the negs tomorrow, and if so, we'll let him. And if he delivers his prints after that we must try to see where he goes. Tomorrow's Saturday. Do you know if they work Saturday mornings in the Archives?'

'No,' said Sally. 'I mean I don't. But Toby's ringing up, so you can ask him.'

'I will. I really don't see that I need tell the police — yet, at any rate. It seems most unlikely that this affair has any connection with Morningside's death, and if it hasn't it's up to the Archives to take any action.'

Sally agreed. Then she told him, reluctantly, about the scene between Toby and Selina, and he looked very anxious.

'Oh, hell,' he said wearily. 'I suppose I shall have to talk to her. Not nice for Toby. Not nice for you. Not nice for any of us.'

Sally went on to Miss Quimper's new information. Johnny listened to it very carefully, and then shook his head. 'It doesn't get us any further,' he said. 'Except that it suggests that Miss Quimper herself is innocent — though Miss Quimper is nobody's fool and there is apparently no confirmation of her story. The fact that Morningside died a few minutes later than we thought makes no difference at all. But I'll go over it with her tomorrow morning — if she's working.'

* * *

TOBY, who rang up after supper and was obviously worried by the Teddy story, said that the Archives staff, generally speaking, worked alternate Saturday mornings. Tomorrow was Teddy's Saturday off — it coincided with Toby's own. Miss Quimper, who was a slow worker and had a tiresome conscience, put in an appearance every Saturday.

Two minutes later the telephone rang again. Johnny, who was still sitting on the arm of Sally's chair, picked up the receiver and gave their number, and Sally listened with him.

A small, precise voice said, 'Is that you, Heldar? Lionel Silcutt speaking. I wonder if I might call on you this evening — quite unofficially, of course — for a few minutes?'

Johnny's eyebrows had gone up. 'Of course, sir,' he said. 'We shall be delighted to see you.'

'You're — er — alone, Heldar? It's a rather confidential matter.'

'There's no one here but ourselves. When may we expect you?'

'I'm at the Club. I can be with you in about a quarter of an hour, if that suits you.'

'Very well indeed, sir. Come along.'

'Thank you, Heldar — thank you. In a quarter of an hour, then. Goodbye.'

'Goodbye, sir.'

Johnny rang off, and Sally asked, 'What on earth do you suppose he wants?'

'I can't imagine. If this were a detective story, he'd be bumped off before he could tell us. It's a classic situation.'

But a quarter of an hour later a taxi drew up at the front door and the bell rang. Johnny went downstairs and brought Silcutt up. He looked even better against the background of the Regency drawing room than he did in the Archives, and he was very uncomfortable and obviously wondering if he ought to have come. Sally did her best, but he couldn't thaw. He refused a drink, coffee, and tea, in that order, and sat on the edge of his chair.

Finally they had to wait for him to speak. He made an obvious effort, swallowed, and began.

'In the course of my duties, Heldar, I have acquired a piece of information which in the last two days has caused me some anxiety. I have at last decided that it is my very distasteful duty to give it to the police, and I should also wish to give it to you — unofficially, you understand.'

'Quite so, sir,' said Johnny gravely.

'It concerns Michael Knox of the Cuttings Department. He has, as perhaps you know, been with us just under a month, and he came to us from the staff of the *Sunday Reflector*. When he applied for this post, he had no written references, and I naturally rang up his late editor. Among the questions I asked was: "Why did he leave the *Reflector*?" The answer was somewhat disconcerting. He had had a serious quarrel with the editor, and had, I gathered, actually used violence. The editor went on — I thought somewhat indiscreetly, although he knows me fairly well — to tell me the subject of the quarrel. Knox had asked him to find a job for a young Irish cousin of his: a boy named Terence Dowd, who apparently has some literary ability. He is, in fact, the author of that rather sordid Irish novel called *Fair City*. The editor interviewed him and discovered — with some difficulty — that he had been dismissed from his last post; he had been teaching English at a prep school on the South coast. I recognised its name and knew that it was a very second-rate establishment. The editor communicated with the headmaster, whose reply was unfavourable. He was obliged to turn the boy down, and Knox was infuriated. He chose to believe, I gathered, that Dowd was being rejected on moral grounds — which with some justification he considered unfair — whereas the editor was really influenced by the headmaster's opinion and his own that the boy was quite unsuited to journalism.

'The matter might have ended there. But, as I told you, I had recognised the name of young Dowd's school. It was, in fact, the school at which Morningside had taught before coming to us. Out of idle curiosity, I asked Morningside what he knew of Dowd. He knew, unfortunately, a good deal.' Silcutt hesitated. *'De mortuis*, Heldar. I knew Morningside better than most of his colleagues did — we formed the nucleus of the Archives personnel, before the place was ever opened. I admired his ability, and in many ways, I liked him very much. But he hadn't been to a public school, poor chap, and he was by nature a prig and a talebearer. He told me he had discovered, in the summer of last year, that young Dowd was — er—' Silcutt looked uneasily at Sally and then made up his mind with difficulty '—was carrying on a passionate and ill-timed affair with the matron, a very young and half-trained girl who in any better-organised school wouldn't have held a position of responsibility. Morningside had felt himself obliged to inform the headmaster, and they had both been dismissed. The following term he himself had resigned; he had never been popular with his colleagues, and as a result of the — er — the *affaire* Dowd' — Silcutt turned rather pink, evidently deciding that the phrase was not as well chosen as he had thought — 'he had become even less so.'

There was another silence. It took Sally some little time to remember that Selina had virtually confessed to having caused Morningside's death. Her reason for bearing him ill-will was still a little obscure, and here was something which, combined with Knox's jealousy, looked more like a motive than anything they had found yet.

Silcutt was looking acutely unhappy. 'I hope,' he said, 'I can trust you not to get this thing out of proportion. Of course it's ridiculous when one really thinks about it. Knox may have an Irish temper, but he's a reputable newspaperman.'

CHAPTER EIGHT

It was ten minutes to eight, and Sally was frying bacon, when she heard the telephone ring. She cursed it, took the frying-pan off the gas, turned out the grill to save the toast, and ran to the door. She was in the hall when Johnny answered the telephone in the drawing room, and she sighed and went back to the kitchen.

A few minutes later Johnny came in. He was in his dressing gown, with a towel round his neck. She knew as soon as she saw his face that something had happened.

'Darling—' she said.

'That was Toby,' he said flatly. 'Miss Quimper is dead.'

He couldn't tell her the story then, for Nanny came down with the children. He told her the bones of it after breakfast, while he finished dressing, but neither of them knew the full details until they heard it from Laxton three-quarters of an hour later. The police had finished with him, for the moment at least, and he was off duty. He sat in Toby's office, large and stolid and youngish, with Toby and Camberley as well as the Heldars listening to him and talked in his steady Yorkshire voice with its broad flat vowels. Only his eyes still showed signs of shock.

'I came off duty as usual at 'alf past seven. I went through Garrick Square, like I always do, and along the path between this building and the bombed site. It runs from the square to St Barnabas' Lane, down below 'ere.' He jerked a broad thumb at the window. 'It was a chilly-like morning, with a bit of a drizzle — a Scotch mist, like. The clouds were low down, and there was no sign of the sun, though it should 'ave been just rising. There's a wooden railing between the path and the bombed site, but it's been rotten for a long time now. I 'appened to look down, and I saw 'er lying there, close in below the path. She was sort of spread-eagled, but 'er 'ead was on its side, and I knew 'er at once. I knew she'd 'ad it, too, the way she was lying. All in among the rubble and the dead willow-'erb, she was. It's about twenty feet down — must 'ave been a double basement — and falling on the stones she could easily 'ave been killed. Or she might 'ave died of exposure during the night.' His eyes widened suddenly.

Camberley said quietly, 'No good brooding, Laxton. You couldn't have known she was there.'

'Did you see her go out?' asked Johnny.

'No, sir. She always goes the front way. I suppose she could 'ave gone out my way while I was looking round outside. That would be a little after six-thirty. Say six-thirty-five to six-forty, same as it was the last time. But even then, I'd 'ave a good chance of seeing 'er if she went through the square. It's a small place, and well lit.'

Johnny left it at that. As it happened, the night-porter at the Fleet Street entrance had been relieved just sufficiently late to hear about Miss Quimper's death, and had stayed, out of curiosity, just sufficiently later to be questioned by Toby, who had arrived at twenty past eight. Miss Quimper hadn't left by his door, so she must, thought Sally, have slipped out by Laxton's while he was on patrol.

'And after you'd found her?' asked Johnny.

'I didn't waste time going down, sir. Even if she 'ad been alive I couldn't 'ave done nothing for 'er. I came straight back to my door — it was quicker than 'unting for a policeman — and got the switchboard to dial nine-nine-nine. Then I phoned Mr Lorn.'

'You couldn't have done better, Laxton.' Camberley looked at Johnny.

'He did exactly right,' said Johnny. 'Tell me, Laxton, did anyone from the Archives leave by your door after you came on duty last night?'

'No, sir. When I came on the day man told me the boys 'ad just gone as usual — we 'ave to keep an eye on them. That Teddy went first, and then the others, a couple of minutes later. But nobody else from the Archives ever goes out our way, except one or two of the girls from the Negatives Department, now and then — so the day man says.'

'Right, Laxton. Thank you. That's all.'

'Go home and try to get some sleep, Laxton,' said Camberley.

'Yes, sir. Thank you, sir.' He got up and went out, and the small office seemed a little less crowded, though Johnny and Camberley between them took up a good deal of it.

Johnny rose too, moved to the window, opened one casement, and looked out and down. Camberley joined him and stood with one foot on the low sill. Johnny said, 'We can't see much from here. I'm going down, if I may. The police seem to have closed the path, but I think I can get some sort of view.'

'I'll come with you,' said Camberley.

Johnny let Sally come too, which showed her that he

was extremely reluctant to leave her in Peex. Toby made a fourth. They went down in the back lift and out by Laxton's door and turned into the little square. It was loud with the rhythmic clatter of printing-presses coming up through the frosted-glass windows of the basement, and the open throttles of the news vans which were pulling out from the ramp on the left. Beyond the ramp was an old grey archway, which led to a very narrow alley running between the back of the *Echo* building and the side of an eighteenth-century house. Under the arch a uniformed constable was standing. He recognised Camberley and saluted.

'Good morning,' said Camberley. 'We don't want to make things awkward for you. May we go along so far?'

'Certainly, sir. It's all right to the end of the concrete, where the trestle is. But it becomes earth after that, so if you don't mind—'

'Of course not. We don't want to mess up any footprints there are.'

'Thank you, sir.'

The trestle stood six or seven paces down the alley. The house came to an end here, and the ground behind it fell away. The alley itself turned into a narrow path with the *Echo* building on its left, and on its right a sheer drop inadequately barred by a mouldering rail, with a wide gap in it a couple of paces beyond the trestle. Twenty yards farther on the path ran into St. Barnabas' Lane. At that point there were a second trestle and a second policeman, who was discouraging a tendency among the passers-by to coagulate along the low parapet.

Sally was so well accustomed to bombed sites that they had ceased to horrify her, except now and then, when she looked at a great area of devastation, and remembered. But this one held horror for her. She looked down into it, below the gap in the railing, and saw a series of white chalk marks, like a frame, on the broken stones. The frame was a most extraordinary shape.

Johnny looked down and up. Then he said, 'I don't think there's anything more to see here. I'd just like to go round to the other side of the site.' He took Sally's arm and walked her back to the square.

Another alley led them out of it on the north side and into a lane which ran along the far side of the site. Johnny stopped on the narrow pavement and looked across the parapet and the crater to the path with the ugly brick wall towering above it. After a moment he said, 'Toby, would Miss Quimper have gone along that path in the dark?'

'Oh, yes, I think so,' said Toby. 'She was very tough — physically — and I imagine quite fearless, and she always wore sensible shoes. And there's a streetlamp on a bracket inside that archway, and another at the St Barnabas' Lane end. The path is a reasonable short-cut on the way to Holborn, if you leave by Laxton's door.'

'Yes,' said Johnny. 'Yes, no doubt.'

'I notice,' said Camberley, 'you don't think this was an accident. Nor do I. I don't like coincidences. Two violent but unconnected deaths within forty-eight hours or so are a bit more than I can swallow.'

'Yes,' said Johnny, with conviction this time. 'And what's more, Miss Quimper died after she'd told Sally that she'd seen Morningside within a minute or two of his death, and before I could question her about it.'

'She told Sally that?' asked Toby. He added abruptly, before either of the Heldars could answer, 'Newshounds over there. Let's get back to Peex before you're recognised.'

They retreated before the advance of a couple of young men in mackintoshes, one of them armed with a camera, and went quickly back through the square. In his office Toby handed round cigarettes, and Johnny told him and Camberley the story of Miss Quimper's first visit to Morningside on the evening of his death, and then asked Sally to repeat the story of the second.

When she had finished Camberley said, 'Yes. I think I can confirm this business of the cutting. It was a *Reflector* editorial on the assassination of the Sultan of Morocco, which I remembered and wanted to refer to for the book I'm doing. I can't remember if I asked Morningside for it when I was in his office in the afternoon, or while we were in the canteen. Can you help me there, Lorn?'

'I don't remember your asking him for a cutting in the canteen, sir.'

'Then it must have been in the afternoon. I ought to have asked Michael Knox for it, of course, but I'd got into a lazy habit of asking Morningside for whatever I wanted for the book — pix or cuts — and leaving him to approach Michael when necessary. I said — or at any rate I meant — that I wanted the thing in the next day or two. But Morningside was always very prompt and conscientious, poor chap. I suppose he had no opportunity of talking to Mike in the afternoon, or perhaps he forgot about it — he had enough on his mind, Heaven knows.' Including, thought Sally, a stand-up row with Mike. It wasn't in the least surprising that Morningside hadn't got round to asking him for cuttings.

'I suppose he remembered it,' Camberley went on, 'while we were all in the canteen, or after he'd left us, and decided to go and look for it himself, before he went into his office, and give it to me when we met at eight. He could cope with the Cuts files, I take it?'

'Oh, yes,' said Toby. 'We're all interchangeable up to a point. It might take him a few minutes, but he'd find it. But' — he turned to Johnny — 'I'm not quite clear about this story. In the first place, I gather Miss

Quimper talked to Sally from this office. Are you suggesting that the conversation was overheard?'

'I think it was,' said Johnny. 'Neither of us repeated
it to anyone here, and I doubt if Miss Quimper would
have made her admission — consciously — to anyone
but Sally or me. I know everyone has normally left by
half past six, but — well, someone came back on
Wednesday evening and killed Morningside.'

'Someone was in Morningside's office,' said Toby,
'while Miss Quimper talked to Sally. You can hear
normal voices through that hatch. They sealed the office for a bit, but it was open again yesterday.'

Sally avoided Johnny's eye. He nodded, and asked,
'Who had the hatch put in, by the way?'

'Not guilty. The original idea was that the man in
this office should have a secretary in Morningside's office, and be able to throw letters and things at her. But I
don't rate a secretary. To continue: I don't see that Miss
Quimper's story was dangerous to the — the murderer.
If she'd told Sally she'd seen someone in Peex at seven-
twenty-five, but didn't want to mention his name over
the telephone, that would have been plain enough.
But—'

Johnny grinned faintly. 'And if she'd said in a low,
urgent voice, "There's someone next door. I must go—"
But you don't get it handed to you on a plate, Toby. I
don't know what there was in her story that was dangerous to the murderer — or that he thought was dangerous to him. He may have been mistaken; acute
anxiety is apt to distort one's sense of proportion. But I
do think he was afraid to let her be questioned about it
by the police and/or me.'

'Fair enough,' said Toby. 'But here's another point.
How could he be sure she'd die? Twenty feet's quite a
fall, but it isn't necessarily fatal. He couldn't even be

sure, in the dark, that she'd fall on stones. Suppose she recovered and gave him away.'

'Yes,' said Johnny. 'That's certainly a point. I don't know.'

He sounded a little abstracted, and Sally diagnosed reluctance to discuss the point. She said, 'And what about the cutting? Where is it now? Miss Quimper said Morningside found it.'

'That's a question,' said Camberley. 'It wasn't visible when we found him. He may have put it in his pocket; I can ask Lindesay about that. I don't think it's in his office — I was in there yesterday afternoon looking for some pix, and I think I'd have noticed it. But we can look.'

They searched Morningside's office carefully, but the cutting wasn't there. Then they went along to Cuts. It was another big room, though not as big as Peex, with one small office for Knox and another for his typists and, in a far corner, a glass-walled cubicle which contained the Archives switchboard.

Knox wandered out of his office as they made their way between the filing cabinets, and Toby said, 'Hullo, Mike. I thought this was your Saturday off.'

'Most of them are,' said Knox, with a warm smile. 'Here next Saturday and here last Saturday — but never here this Saturday. Well, hardly ever.' Then the smile faded.

'My principal assistant,' he said, clipping his words, 'rang me up and told me about Miss Quimper. If I can help you at all, Heldar, please tell me. I never got on with Miss Quimper, but she was a good woman.'

'Thank you,' said Johnny. 'On Wednesday afternoon, did Morningside by any chance speak to you about a *Reflector* cutting he wanted for Brigadier Camberley?'

'No,' said Knox.

'According to Miss Quimper, he looked for it himself in your files about half past seven on Wednesday evening, found it, and went back to Peex with it. Will you look in your files now and see if by any chance it's there?'

Johnny glanced at Camberley, who provided the particulars. Knox made an Irish noise which seemed to signify comprehension, strode away, squatted down before a filing cabinet, opened the bottom drawer, and began to separate the files in it. After a few moments his long fingers came up, delicately holding a big cutting. He closed the drawer, straightened himself, strode back, and gave the cutting to Camberley. 'This it?' he asked.

Camberley looked at it. 'Yes, that's it,' he said. 'Did you expect this, Heldar?'

'No,' said Johnny slowly. 'No, I didn't. I think, sir, it had better go to Lindesay.'

'Fool that I am!' said Camberley. 'I've probably messed up any fingerprints there are.' He laid the cutting carefully on the top of the nearest filing cabinet.

'I doubt if there are any, you know.' Johnny turned back to Knox. 'Any use asking you what you were doing about six-thirty yesterday evening?'

'I was at home.'

'Where do you live?'

'Top flat at Fifteen Crawley Street, Bloomsbury. I live alone. I got home about a quarter past six, having had a quickish drink in Fleet Street first. When you saw me at five-thirty I was on my way to it. I dare say the barmaid might remember me, but that wouldn't give me an alibi for six-thirty. The Belgian couple who live below me may have heard me come in, but they're the most frightful liars, and I'm afraid they like me.'

'Any further comment on Wednesday evening?'

'Sorry,' said Knox, and smiled warmly again.

'Michael,' said Camberley quietly, 'you're a hell of a

poseur. But you're not a fool, and you know your world. You know damn well that if your story isn't relevant it won't have to come out. If it's completely irrelevant I don't suppose Heldar will even repeat it to the police, unless he has to do it for your sake. On the other hand, of course' — he looked very straight at Knox — 'if you won't tell it I should say you're almost bound to get into trouble.'

'I've been in trouble before now,' said Knox, with another smile.

'I know you have. I've been in trouble with you, which makes me foolishly reluctant to see you in it again.'

'That's very good of you. But please don't worry.'

'That's easier said than done. All right, Mike. It's no use pressing you.'

Knox's eyes rested on the Brigadier with a curious expression, which Sally couldn't quite read. It seemed to be partly sardonic and partly rather unhappy.

They went back to Toby's office. Camberley said a little abruptly, 'I'm sorry that didn't work. Michael was a War Correspondent in the desert while I was there, and I got to know him pretty well. He seems almost like one of my own boys. But he hasn't been quite the same lately.'

Sally remembered that Knox had been slating Camberley in the *Reflector*. He was evidently an iconoclast, but it seemed a pity he had had to pick on someone so inherently generous. It was perhaps understandable that Camberley preferred not to ask him for cuttings.

CHAPTER NINE

They settled down to wait for Lindesay, who was supposed to be coming back to question the Saturday staff. It was after half past eleven when he appeared, and they gathered that he had been seeing the girls in Miss Quimper's department, the two messengers on duty, and the people in Cuttings.

He took Sally first and listened to Miss Quimper's story. He looked rather more austere than before, and she was glad when he released her. She wasn't allowed to rejoin the others in Toby's office. But there was no objection to her waiting for Johnny, and the young plain-clothes man who had been left outside in Peex shepherded her to a table. Camberley was taken next. A quarter of an hour later he came out, and Johnny was fetched. Camberley paused beside Sally.

'Will you forgive me if I don't wait?' he asked. 'I've got to meet someone for lunch.'

It was five minutes after that that she heard the low voices of two assistants behind the nearest row of filing cabinets. (Selina wasn't here this morning; as Toby's principal assistant she obviously wouldn't be off duty on his Saturday off.)

One girl said, 'When do you suppose we'll get away? I wanted to catch a train at ten past one.'

The other said, 'Well, at this rate, I doubt if you'll do it.'

'I ought to ring up, then. I was counting on getting off at half past twelve as usual.'

Sally looked automatically at her watch. It was close on twenty-five past twelve. It flashed suddenly upon her that Teddy would presumably be leaving the building at half past and might make straight for his client.

She got up without thinking and smiled at the young plain-clothes man.

'Would you be very kind,' she said, 'and tell my husband I couldn't wait after all?'

'Certainly, Mrs Heldar.' He smiled too.

'It's the photographs we had to pick up,' she added hurriedly, and moved on. 'I'll be home as soon as I can.'

'I'll tell him, Mrs Heldar; don't worry.' He came with her to open one of the glass doors. She thanked him warmly and went on.

She ran along the passage and pressed the down button of the nearer lift. Everyone must have been too busy with the police for the last hour or two to send Teddy out on jobs or to organise him at all. He might not have been able to replace the Venezuelan negs, but he could probably have left the building half an hour ago without anyone's noticing — anyone except the day-porter at Laxton's door. The lift, according to the indicator, was at the ground floor and not moving. Sally, growing reckless, pressed the down button of the next one, which was at the second. But the nearer lift came first. The doors opened with their usual maddening decorum, and she went in and pressed the ground-floor button.

He might well have gone, she thought, as she hurried out on to the crowded pavement. If he hadn't, he wouldn't be long. But she hadn't got a newspaper, and she would probably have to go to the corner of St Barnabas' Lane to get one. She couldn't risk that. She was wearing a scarf over her head, so at least her hair was hidden. She would get into the doorway Johnny had used yesterday afternoon — unless the restaurant was open...

Teddy emerged suddenly from Thrale Passage, and turned towards her. She turned abruptly herself, stared into the *Echo*'s display window, and saw his reflection pass her. Then she began to follow him.

She had never done such a thing in her life. It was very rash indeed; he was almost bound to look round and see her. But this might be their only chance; he evidently wasn't going home to the King's Cross neighbourhood.

He turned into St Barnabas' Lane, walking so fast that she had her work cut out to keep him in sight. Presently he crossed the narrow, traffic-filled street almost under the bows of a news van. The driver leaned out and swore at him, but the incident gave Sally a little confidence. He was thinking only of getting wherever he was going.

He turned into Holborn and increased his pace on the wider pavement. Sally began to trot. They proceeded in this way for a quarter of a mile. Then Teddy's red head disappeared down the steps of Chancery Lane Station.

She felt in her bag for coppers and seized a newspaper as she passed the news-stand at the top. Then she followed Teddy down. She was convinced for a moment that this was a trick, that he was waiting round the corner to find out if she was following him. But when she swung round it, she saw the red head in the queue at the booking-office. She was just near enough, when he reached the window, to hear him ask for a single to Belsize Park. Presumably he would go home from there when his business was done.

She asked for the same thing. By the time she reached the top of the first escalator he was near the foot of it, clattering down fast. He hurried straight on to the second, which led to the westbound platform. Sally put on a spurt, and reached the platform just as a train came in. Any train would be right. She saw the red head in the crowd but made no attempt to get into the same carriage. Better not. In a crowd like this she wouldn't be able to move. She would probably be hidden from him, but she couldn't hide. If he knew she was following him and Belsize Park was a bluff, she would lose him. But if it wasn't a bluff, it would be all right as long as she was on the same train. Only she mustn't get too far behind during the change at Tottenham Court Road.

She stood jam-packed as the train rattled through the darkness. Only two stops this time. First Holborn, and then the darkness again. Then the second lighted platform. The doors slid open again. She got out, looked for the way to the Northern Line, found it, and discovered the red head between her and it.

It was quite a long way. Through to the eastbound platform and along it, up and down short flights of steps, along passages, round corners, and finally on to the southbound platform and through to the northbound. Then there was a wait. Sally didn't know this line well, and she had to read the indicator and the map with her newspaper raised between her and Teddy. They wanted an Edgware train, and that would be the second one in. She retired to the entry by which she had come and stood there behind the paper. When the second train stopped, she walked forward, looking awkwardly for her way on the safe side, and dived in.

She found a seat, and was able to relax a little, but not much. She had been once to Belsize Park Station, and to the best of her recollection there were lifts. If she let Teddy go up and took the next lift, she would probably lose him. If she took the same lift, he would probably recognise her.

They had reached the station before she had made up her mind. She had realised that not very many people were likely to get off here, and she took it slowly. Teddy and two other people were well on their way, and the doors were about to close, when she slipped out and followed. Up a flight of steps, across a bridge.

Mercifully there was no waiting outside. The lift was there. Sally took a desperate decision, pulled her scarf farther over her face and, with her newspaper in position, walked in. The woman who took her ticket told her to look where she was going, and she mumbled an apology. The doors shut, and the lift started with a jerk.

When it stopped, she waited till the doors had opened, and then risked a glance at the further end. Teddy was already out. She followed again, her newspaper still up, and from the cover of the station exit watched him cross the busy road, turn to the right past a line of shops on the far side, and then turn off to the left. She shot across the road and ran. When she reached the corner, she looked round it, and to her relief saw him fifty yards down the side road.

There were very few other people in sight. But she remembered that Teddy had never seen the coat she was wearing, and that her face was invisible except from the front. She was on the point of crossing the road when Teddy did it himself.

Presently he turned into another road, flanked by small red-brick houses, with plane trees growing at the kerbs. After that he turned three times in fairly quick succession, walking faster and faster and never looking back. She followed on the other pavement, running when he had disappeared, always afraid of losing him.

At last she rounded a corner just in time to see him turn in, twenty yards ahead of her, at a little gateway in a low wall from which the railings had gone. It wasn't the gate which led to the steps and the high porch of the semi-detached grey stuccoed house, but a side gate beyond that. He dived down what must be another flight of steps between the house and its further neighbour and vanished again.

Sally walked straight on, noting the name of the road and the number of the house. Beside the basement gate a name was painted in cobalt-blue letters on the top of the low wall: 'Hilary Longwall'.

At the next corner she turned and waited, half-hidden by a higher wall. She had waited perhaps three minutes when Teddy reappeared and turned towards the station. She stood still for a moment, undecided. Then she made up her mind. Better let well alone. She was quite certain he had delivered his prints. Nothing but business, surely, could have brought him so far off his usual beat — and apparently without his lunch, too. She was feeling the strain, and it would be a pity to slip up now. She gave him two minutes' law, and then walked slowly back to the station. She didn't catch up with him.

There would be call boxes in the station, but she had to stop and buy cigarettes at a small café opposite before she had enough pennies. It was twenty-five past one. She assumed that Johnny had interpreted her hurried message correctly and gone home. She put the pennies in and dialled. The telephone rang once. Then she heard him say, 'Hullo,' and pressed Button A.

'Johnny,' she said, 'listen. I've found Teddy's client. I'm at Belsize Park Underground Station. At least, I shall be in a little café opposite, if you want to come.'

'I'll come,' he said. 'Tell me exactly what you've found, will you?'

She told him. 'I think the name's familiar,' she said when she had finished, 'only I can't place it. Can you?'

'Not at the moment. What's the name of this café?'

She remembered it and told him.

'All right,' he said. 'If you leave it before I get there, I'll beat you. I'm not sure I shan't do it anyway. Goodbye.'

She went over to the café and ordered sausages and chips. She was halfway through them when she was struck by the frightful idea that Hilary Longwall might be an honest-to-goodness client of the Archives, and that Teddy might have been sent to him — or her — in the course of duty. She didn't really think so, but she would never live such a thing down.

She was eating biscuits and cheese and drinking coffee when Johnny came in. It was only a quarter to two, so he had probably taken a taxi. She had guessed from his voice over the telephone that he had been really anxious, and as soon as she saw him, she knew it. She knew too that she had been a little frightened. He sat down beside her, and she said in a small voice, 'I'm sorry.'

The café was quite empty except for themselves. Johnny took her hand and said quietly, 'Never again. That's an order. Understand?'

'Yes,' she said. Then the waitress reappeared, found them holding hands, and was obviously delighted. Johnny ordered the sausages and chips, and she brought him a fried egg as well.

When he had reached the coffee stage, he gave Sally a cigarette, lit one for himself, and got down to business, speaking low again.

'I rang up Toby about the name you mentioned. I gathered from your message that you would come home when you could, and that if you wanted to communicate you would probably communicate with home, but Toby stayed on his office telephone just in case. And, incidentally, I'm ashamed of you, vamping plain-clothes men.'

'How do you know I did?'

'The poor boy was all dewy-eyed when he gave me your message. Anyway, I rang up Toby, and his Fleet Street memory produced the information we wanted. Your discovery is the young man who went into Hungary during the October Revolution — which the Archives, for filing purposes, call the Hungarian Rising. At least, he said he went in. Since he didn't travel with any other students, and didn't meet anyone who could identify him afterwards, there is some uncertainty about it. The *Sunday Echo* bought his story, but the more sober newspapers were a bit chary. He got back to Cambridge halfway through the following term, but was let off with a caution — possibly, I imagine, because the authorities didn't want to pander to his self-importance by giving him any more publicity. But he went off to the Venezuelan Revolution last January, and that finished his University career. At least, he said he'd been to Venezuela. Again there would seem to be no witnesses, though the *Sunday Echo* took him up that time, too.'

'Of course,' said Sally. 'I remember the story now. Are we going to see him?'

'Yes, I don't see why you shouldn't come. He doesn't sound a very formidable proposition. I think, by the way, I know why he wanted to buy the pix privately. It wasn't just that he was looking for a bargain, and in fact he probably paid more than the Archives' price. It was rather silly of me not to see the client's motive before.'

He explained the client's motive as they walked back through the suburban roads. Presently they came to the wide avenue with the grey stuccoed houses. Johnny grimaced at the sight of the cobalt name. 'My God, what affectation!' he said, and followed Sally down the narrow flight of steps and into a messy little courtyard occupied by dustbins and smelling slightly of household refuse. In the wall of the house there was a cobalt door, rather dirty, and the name of Hilary Longwall appeared again, in the usual medium, on the stucco beside it.

Johnny rang, and they waited. After a moment or two footsteps sounded inside, and the door was opened. A young man stood there — he was obviously young, in spite of his drab and rather ill-nourished beard; there was something very immature about him. His lank mouse-coloured hair was untidy and hadn't been cut for some time. He was short and squat, and wore a red and green striped shirt, green corduroy slacks, and a pair of extremely vivid sandals.

'Hullo,' he said sulkily. 'What can I do for you?' It was a faintly Cockney voice, and a little husky.

'Mr Longwall?' asked Johnny. 'The author?'

'Yes,' said the young man. 'Have you come about my book? I've more or less fixed up with Ovingdon's, but come in and have a drink and we'll talk it over. I haven't actually signed the contract yet, you know; I'm not altogether satisfied with the terms they're offering.'

Johnny accepted the invitation. Murmuring polite thanks, he got himself and Sally into the house before Longwall had stopped talking. They found themselves in a dark passage and slipped through an open doorway into a room at the back of the house.

The walls had been painted white, some time ago. The curtains and the rugs which lay on the worn linoleum looked to Sally like Latin American Brummagem. The furniture was cheap and ugly and rather sparse. There were a good many books, on shelves and elsewhere; most of them seemed to be political works of the Labour persuasion, but some were on Hungary and Latin America. A portable typewriter stood uncovered on a table, with a quarto sheet in it and a pile of papers beside it. There were two or three prints on the walls, all, apparently, of contemporary pictures, and to Sally almost incomprehensible. Everything was covered with dust, and the floor round the table was deep in crumpled paper.

'Have a drink,' said Longwall, picking up a bottle of wine from the mantelpiece. 'This is Jugo-Slav, and quite good.'

'No, thank you,' said Johnny politely, and Sally refused too.

'No? Sit down, then.' He left them to find seats for themselves and dropped on to a divan covered with an already crumpled and rather unconvincing poncho-type blanket. 'Now, about my book. It isn't finished, of course, but I can give you a précis. Personal experiences of that type have a very big sale, as you know, especially when they're decently written. And I've got some astounding original photographs. You'll see them on the table there.'

Johnny, who had put Sally into an uncomfortable armchair and was fetching for himself the straight chair in front of the typewriter, picked up the large, glossy prints and looked at them.

'Very interesting,' he said. He brought the chair over and sat down with the photographs in his hand. 'Unfortunately, I'm not a publisher.'

Longwall's jaw dropped. 'Then why did you say you were?' he demanded.

'I didn't, you know,' said Johnny. 'You assumed I was.'

'Then who the hell are you?'

'My name's Heldar. I'm a bookseller by trade, but at the moment I'm acting as a private enquiry agent for the National Press Archives. Tell me, did you really imagine you could publish these pictures as your own and get away with it?'

Longwall began to stammer, and Johnny cut him short. 'At the best it would have been a big risk. Anyone in the Archives and quite a number of newspapermen might have recognised them. But since there's a certain amount of doubt about your visits to Hungary and Venezuela your publishers would probably have gone rather carefully into the origin of the pictures before using them, and even if they'd decided it was safe there would have been enquiries after publication. You would certainly have been caught out one way or another. What did you pay Parston for them?'

The battle was comparatively short. Longwall became furious and tried to bluff it out. Johnny kept his temper and remained entirely unimpressed. Longwall's fury merged into the technical Angry Young Man attitude and embraced the world at large and all those responsible for it. Johnny waited patiently. Longwall passed from anger to plaintiveness and, when that had no effect, to sulks, and still Johnny waited. Finally, when the wheel seemed to have come full-circle, he put his question again.

'Five guineas each,' said Longwall. 'He wouldn't take less. I didn't tell him what I wanted them for, of course, but—'

'But it was obvious to him that you wanted them quite badly. And it didn't strike you that you were putting yourself in his hands?' Johnny ran through the prints as he spoke. Even in his fury Longwall hadn't attempted to take them back. Johnny's ex-Commando physique and obviously first-class condition didn't invite liberties.

'Eleven,' he said. 'Was that all this lot?'

'Yes. Those were all that were good enough.'

'Or the pick of those that hadn't been published. Nearly sixty pounds on them. And the Hungarian ones?'

'Fifteen at the same price,' said Longwall sullenly.

'I see. One hundred and thirty-six pounds ten in all. I don't know that it was particularly generous, considering what you obviously hoped to make out of the book, and what you must have been paid by the *Sunday Echo* for your adventures. You gave the boy cash, I suppose? Yes. Well, I'll take the Hungarian lot as well.'

'If I give them to you, will you advise the Archives not to take any action?'

'Don't be silly,' snapped Johnny. 'The Archives will do as they think best. They may prosecute themselves, or the copyright-holders may do it — or both. What is absolutely certain is that someone will take you to court if you don't return all these prints. And I imagine the *Echo* will be rather annoyed too. If it comes out that you've gone as far as this to bolster up your story, they're going to look awful fools.'

Longwall, rather white now, got another sheaf of prints out of the table drawer, and Johnny counted them. Then he said, 'Where did you meet Parston?'

Longwall hesitated, and the colour came back into his face. 'At a dance at the Clerkenwell Palais,' he said. 'A fortnight ago.'

'Quite so. *Nostalgie de la boue*, I suppose. Did he bring the Venezuelan pictures out here on Wednesday evening?'

'No. I was in the Fleet Street neighbourhood any-way, and he met me in a pub — the Grapevine. It's quite close to the *Echo* building. He brought the finished Hungarian prints, and the Venezuelan pictures for me to choose from. I made him bring the whole file in both cases. I couldn't trust him to make any sort of selection.'

'What time did he arrive?'

'Just before seven. He was due at seven. He only stayed a few minutes. I would have liked to take a bit longer over my selection, but he was in a great hurry, and very jumpy. Someone had found out a bit about what he was doing and threatened to give him away. He told me about it, actually, when we fixed up the meeting at the pub on the telephone — that was on Monday evening. He'd been caught putting back the pictures — the Hungarian pictures — on Monday at lunchtime. He wasn't keen to meet me again and get the Venezuelan prints made for me, but he said he would if this chap didn't give him away in the meantime. He wanted the money, obviously — I suppose it was a for-tune for him. The man who caught him wasn't black-mailing him — he was apparently considering whether it was his duty to report him.' Longwall's voice was de-liberately pompous. 'The prefect type, it would seem.'

'What was his name?' asked Johnny.

'The man's? Mornington, Morningside — some-thing like that—'

Longwall broke off. 'My God,' he said, and put a hand to his mouth. 'That — that's the chap—'

'You do read the papers occasionally, then,' said Johnny.

Longwall was too shaken to notice the sarcasm. 'Yes. I never thought of it till now. But I remember — I re-member now — Parston was very jittery, but he said he could deal with Morningside. I thought he was just showing off, but—'

The Heldars left Hilary Longwall, rather thankfully, and climbed up to the road. Johnny looked a little sick.

'I've never in my life,' he said, 'met anyone quite so self-centred. The moment he assumed without the faintest justification that we'd come after his book, I knew we were off, but I didn't expect him to keep it up from beginning to end without a break. I'm sorry I took you.'

'It was rather interesting,' said Sally.

'Ill-mannered cub,' said Johnny, and the old-fashioned epithet seemed entirely appropriate. 'He gave Teddy away with both hands, too. Obviously, Morningside didn't know the whole truth, or he'd have reported Teddy without hesitation. But an investigation would have brought it all out, and that would have meant the sack, and perhaps prosecution. We know now what Teddy meant when he said to Morningside, "Wotcher goin' ter do abaht it? That's wot I wanter know." From your description that sounded unusually urgent and persistent for a piece of ordinary rudeness, and Teddy sounded unusually upset. And Morningside said he hadn't decided, but if Teddy went on that way, he'd get what was coming to him.'

'Yes, and that was why he was looking for Morningside the day before. Morningside had slept on it, and he might have decided. And Teddy was anxious enough to forget that he'd be at lunch.'

'Teddy hadn't very long,' said Johnny. 'On Wednesday evening, I mean. Even if he left Longwall at five past seven, he had to get back to Echo House, in by the coal-hole in Garrick Square, and up to Peex, and do the job and get away by twenty past at the latest. I suppose it's just possible.'

After a moment Sally asked, 'What about alibis for last night? We know Michael Knox hasn't got one.'

'Toby hasn't either. He left Echo House about six, went back to his flat, and stayed there.'

'That doesn't matter. He's got one for Morningside.'

'Yes. I don't know about the others yet, but Toby's going to do his best to find out. In the meantime' — Johnny looked extremely uncomfortable — 'I think I must see Selina. I'll ring her up when we get home.'

CHAPTER TEN

B ut when they got home Selina was there. Nanny, with unerring instinct, had recognised her as one of the original employer class, and had put her in the drawing room and lit the fire. She stood up as they walked in, tall and graceful in a long tweed coat, half in shadow because the November afternoon was closing in, half seen in the flickering firelight, which struck gold pieces out of her hair and turned her eyes to enormous pits of shadow.

'I do hope you'll forgive me, Mrs Heldar,' she said. She hadn't lost her poise, but her clear voice lacked a little of its usual assurance. 'I was rather uncertain about coming, and when your Nanny said you were out, I nearly ran away. But she made up my mind for me.'

'I'm very glad she did,' said Sally. 'She said you'd been waiting nearly half an hour, so we must apologise for being so long. Do sit down and let Johnny entertain you while I get some tea.'

She had kept her own poise, such as it was. It was easier not to think that she might have in her house the woman who had killed Morningside and Miss Quimper — a woman who was attractive but insane.

She had been forced to think so seriously about Michael Knox and Teddy that the impact of Selina's admission had diminished a little, and she was confused.

When she went upstairs with the tray Selina and Johnny were talking about the new play at the Sphere. Johnny got up and took the tray from her, and then went downstairs to fetch the cakes and the buttered toast. It was quite clear that he hadn't joined issue with Selina yet.

If Nanny had looked in, she would have thought it a very comfortable tea party. Sally had turned on the lamps and drawn the curtains. Everyone had a reasonably good appetite, and everyone talked. Selina, perhaps, talked a shade too much. But there was no other sign of strain.

When they had finished, Johnny passed the cigarette-box to Selina and then to Sally. He lit their cigarettes and his own. Then he looked at Selina and said, 'Well?'

She said slowly, 'Toby rang me up at lunchtime and told me about Miss Quimper, and Inspector Lindesay came to see me this afternoon. I'm frightfully sorry, and I'd like to do anything I can to help. But I'm not pretending to be entirely altruistic. This second — I suppose one's got to call it murder — has brought things to a head for me. I've been trying to make myself come to you ever since Thursday morning. I know I'm a suspect. I knew I was going to be. The police discovered that I was engaged to Frank, and I can't tell them all about it because they wouldn't understand. They also discovered that I lied to them when I said I'd gone home just after six on Wednesday evening and stayed there. They know I went back to the Archives a little before seven. And now they know that I haven't got an alibi for Miss Quimper. I left the Archives at twenty to six and went home and stayed there — I really did this time — but the girl I share with went home for the weekend — she went straight to the station from her office — so I've got nobody to swear to it.'

She was obviously anxious now, and a little breathless. Her face was flushed by eagerness and the hot fire beside her, and she looked very lovely.

'And you can explain it all to us?' asked Johnny.

'Not easily,' she said. 'Things of this kind are very difficult to talk about to anyone, and I made a frightful fool of myself. But it's far easier to tell you and your wife than the police.'

'You realise,' said Johnny quietly, 'that I can't undertake to keep anything you may tell me from the police?'

'Yes. I realise you're a responsible person. You can use it as you like, if only you can sort things out.'

'I'll do my best. Will you go on?'

She didn't answer for quite a long time. 'I'm not quite sure myself,' she said at last, 'why I got engaged to Frank. It was partly reaction, I think. My mother is a twenty-horse-power snob, and I had a good deal of difficulty in prising myself out of the county background and going to Oxford and getting a job. I got engaged — at least half-consciously — to annoy her, and because I thought I wanted to cut my ties with the life I'd left. But at the same time, though I didn't see it then, I was looking for some sort of compensation. The county background may be tiresome, but at least it's secure and permanent, and when I'd renounced it, I felt lost. Frank and his background seemed satisfactorily solid and reliable — at the time I saw them as much more solid and reliable than anything I'd left. And much more worthwhile. I thought Frank had all the virtues that my own kind — generally speaking — lacked. In his world everyone was strictly sober and faithful and church-going. I thought that was what I wanted in a man. So when Frank asked me rather formally and restrainedly to marry him, I said I would.

'But it didn't work, of course. Frank had the — the defects of his qualities, though it's hardly fair to call them defects, and anyway I should have seen them long before I got engaged to him; everyone else did. He was smug and priggish, and he had no sense of humour. And then—'

Selina stopped for a moment and put her hands up to her temples. 'It wasn't particularly reasonable of me to mind all that — after all, it was my fault I was engaged to it. But it was far worse to mind his being non-U — crude and not properly educated and having an accent and not knowing his world. I felt such a beast all the time. It wasn't his fault, and I'd no right to quarrel with it when I'd got myself into it. At the same time I was having hell with my mother — mostly at a distance. I couldn't bring myself to take Frank home, and he knew damned well why, and Mummy guessed. And yet I was so pigheaded about it I couldn't break it off.

'We'd been engaged for nearly a month when Michael Knox gave a bottle-party. That was soon after he came to the Archives. Frank didn't approve of that sort of party — he never drank — but he had to go because it was for us. That was Michael's devilish ingenuity; he wanted to see Frank at a wild party.'

'And also, possibly, to show you Frank at a wild party?' asked Johnny.

'Yes — I think so. How did you know?'

'Various indications,' said Johnny vaguely. 'Go on.'

'Well, if that was what he wanted it worked. Frank refused all drink, and tried to make me do the same, and I was so annoyed that I got tight and behaved very badly. I wasn't the only one; it was that kind of party. But it was a beastly thing to do to Frank. He left Toby to take me home, and in the morning — it was Sunday

— he left a note in my letterbox saying he really couldn't go on being engaged to me after what had happened. That was a little over a fortnight before he was killed. We had to go on seeing each other, of course, but he was slightly condescending and confined himself strictly to business. As time went on, he became a little more friendly, and I realised that he was beginning to talk almost as if we were still engaged. He didn't make any other advances, but then he wouldn't. Even outside the Archives he'd always been extremely decorous, and I suppose that had irritated me too. Which was unreasonable of me again,' said Selina with an effort, 'because I didn't really want him to break loose. Anyhow, this new change worried me, because I — I didn't want to be engaged to him again. I thought about it all over Wednesday. I was trying to decide whether I ought to leave it alone or have it out with him, and it was only when I was nearly back at the flat that I decided to have it out. It sounds rather bloody, but I really decided it because of that scene he had with Mike.' She looked at Sally. 'You heard it — you couldn't help hearing it. I wondered how I could conceivably have wanted to tie myself up for life with someone who knew so little about it. Anyway, I knew he nearly always worked late on Wednesdays. So I got on to another bus and went back. I slipped in by the Fleet Street entrance about ten to seven. The night-porter was talking to some people, and I hoped afterwards he hadn't noticed me, but he must have done.

'When I got to Peex there was no one there. But Frank hadn't locked his office — I suppose he thought there was no point, at a time when the joker could use his own key without being seen — and his overcoat was there. So I knew he was coming back, and I assumed he was in the canteen. I wandered about his office and looked at one or two of the old negs he was working on, and generally fiddled about; I was pretty restless by then. Frank didn't come up till about twenty past seven. He looked pleased to see me and not in the least surprised. He said in his smuggest voice, "So you've come to say you're sorry. I thought you would. Very well, my dear; I'm sure you've learnt your lesson, and if you'll promise me, you'll never touch alcohol again we'll say no more about it. Here's your ring." He fished it out of his pocket in its box, and then he added, "I've quite decided now that you haven't had anything to do with all these nasty things that have been happening to me. I couldn't have been sufficiently at fault to fall in love with a girl of that sort."

'Well, I saw red. I called him all sorts of things which shocked him very much, and I wish I hadn't now. It's rather frightful to think that he was killed so soon after. Anyway, I left him after three or four minutes. When I passed through the hall the porter wasn't there — and as it happened, I'd used the far lift both going up and coming down, and there's no man on it in the evening. So I was encouraged to tell the police I hadn't come back.'

She stopped and lay back in her chair. The lamplight was kind, but she looked white and strained.

A full minute passed before Johnny spoke. Then he said gravely, 'Thank you, Miss Marvell. I'm sorry, but this story must go to the police. All of it, I'm afraid. The last part is the more important, of course, but the first part must go with it to explain it.'

'All right,' said Selina. 'If you insist. I feel better about it now I've told you. But I don't suppose the police will believe it. I won't ask if you do. You'll want notice of that question.'

'I'm inclined to believe it,' said Johnny. 'At the risk of looking foolish, I'll even say that I'm inclined to admire your courage in telling it. As for the police, the main thing is that they should hear it, and as soon as possible. I'm going to ring up Scotland Yard and ask if I may bring you in at once. I hope Lindesay will be sent for if he's not there.'

* * *

JOHNNY DIDN'T COME BACK till half past six. He had waited for Selina at Scotland Yard and taken her home. He looked a little tired and seemed quite glad to give the case a rest till after supper. Sally decided that it was a night for coffee, and he accepted his cup gratefully, and lit a cigarette. Then he said, 'You see why Selina's story is so important, if it's true?'

'Yes,' said Sally. 'Though I admit the penny didn't drop till you were just leaving. We've been assuming all this time that the booby-trap was rigged while Morningside was in the canteen, between twenty to seven and twenty past. But if Selina's story is true, she was wandering about his office till twenty past. So an alibi for the canteen period isn't the slightest good, and I suppose the trap must have been rigged while he was in Cuts, though that wouldn't give the murderer very long.'

'No,' said Johnny. 'I think we want a timetable.'

He fetched a pad from Sally's desk, and she went and sat beside him on the sofa. Between them they made a detailed table. All their times were approximate, but that couldn't be helped.

6.35 Miss Quimper enters Peex by back way.

6.38 Teddy enters Echo House by Laxton's door.

6.39 Morningside leaves Peex by front way for canteen. Miss Quimper leaves Peex by back way and enters Ladies'.

6.41 Teddy enters Peex by back way.

6.45 Miss Quimper leaves Ladies' and enters back lift.

6.47 Miss Quimper leaves back lift on ground floor. (Laxton's evidence.)

6.50 Selina enters Echo House by Fleet Street entrance. (Brown's evidence.)

6.52 Teddy leaves Peex by back way. (It may have taken him approximately 10 minutes to find the Venezuelan pix; if it hasn't, his date with Longwall is not till 7.00pm, and the Grapevine is close at hand.)

6.53 Selina enters Peex by front way.

6.55 Teddy leaves Echo House by Laxton's door. (Laxton's evidence.)

7.20 Morningside enters Peex by front way from canteen.

7.24 Selina leaves Peex by front way.

7.26 Morningside leaves Peex by back way and enters Cuts.

7.27 Selina leaves Echo House by Fleet Street entrance.

7.30 Miss Quimper enters Cuts.

7.32 Morningside leaves Cuts and re-enters Peex by back way. Miss Quimper leaves Cuts and re-enters back lift.

7.37 Miss Quimper leaves Echo House by Fleet Street entrance. (Brown's evidence?)

'Yes,' said Johnny. 'I think it was long enough. Morningside was probably in Cuts for five or six minutes — he was coping with unfamiliar files — and possibly for as much as nine or even ten, if he left Peex the moment Selina had left it, and if he talked to Miss Quimper for more than two minutes. She said she was with him for a couple of minutes; that might well mean three, and possibly four. And while he was in Cuts the murderer slipped into Peex — I should think by the back way, which is the less public. He probably saw the light on in Cuts, guessed Morningside was there, did the job as quickly as possible, and left by the front way. And, of course, he could leave the lift before the ground floor and find another way out.' He paused, and then went slowly on.

'If Selina is lying, she rigged the trap herself, between six-fifty-three and seven-twenty — plenty of time there. We can almost certainly rule out the possibility of an accomplice. And if she knows that you — or someone — overheard her little scene with poor Toby, she may have designed her story to explain it away. Toby's remark about 'what she did to Morningside that evening' could refer to her behaviour at Knox's party as well as to Morningside's death. In fact, Sally, a good deal better. Remembering how Morningside died, and how shaken Toby was by the sight of his body — and remembering that Toby is very genuinely religious — I can't believe he could ever have brought himself to say that he had no feelings about Morningside's death, however much in love he might have been with the killer. Besides, Selina would have had to be damned sure of his devotion to proceed to a second murder, knowing that he knew she had done the first. She's accustomed to devotion, of course — Toby, Morningside in his way, Knox in his, and apparently even Silcutt. But she's not a fool. I'm quite sure she was talking about Knox's party when you overheard her, and when she spoke of confessing to Toby, she was probably just having a dig at his clerical background. But she may have realised that the scene could be interpreted differently, and she'd be more likely to see that if she had in fact killed Morningside.' Johnny paused again.

'I've been realising very gradually,' he said, 'that Morningside's murder might not be the kind of murder we thought it at all. We thought it the work of an unbalanced person — a dangerous lunatic — who had been feeding his hatred of Morningside with increasingly unpleasant tricks and increasingly nasty communications until it reached proportions so great that he didn't care whether he killed Morningside or not. Or, perhaps, whether he killed anyone else or not. It was as callous and brutal and cold-blooded as you like, but it wasn't an altogether deliberate murder, and it wasn't necessarily backed by any understandable motive.

'Several things made me wonder if we were right. First, there was the apparently deliberate use of Pat's and Pam's rude rhymes and Teddy's prep school tricks as a foundation for the heavier stuff which followed, and, secondly, there was the acquisition of the key to Morningside's office. A madman can be extremely clever, but these things — to my mind — struck an unexpectedly practical and purposeful note which was held throughout the performance. Thirdly, it was clear that the key had been acquired either by Teddy or by the writer of the ruder rhymes, and that the owner of the key was responsible for the booby-trap. Teddy's tricks might have been a stage on the road to lunacy — I'm not a psychiatrist, and I wouldn't know — but they obviously weren't at all necessarily so. On the other hand, the ruder rhyme Toby showed me seemed a perfectly sane production. I got him to repeat to me what he could remember of the others, and it only confirmed my impression. It seemed to me that there was a big gap between those things and the filth of the letters — an even bigger gap than there was between Teddy's prep school stuff and the poltergeist tricks, if only because the rhymes were obviously the work of a mature mind and the prep school stuff — in this case — the work of an adolescent one. When I said so to Toby, he reminded me that the rhymes had shaded off gradually, and that the only one I had actually seen had been an early effort. But I wasn't quite convinced. I was beginning to think that what had been presented to us might be not the real degeneration of a good mind, but a deliberate impression of it. Not a perfect impression, perhaps, but about as good as it could be, given a definite starting-point which must have seemed too good to waste, but which involved the impressionist in a rather tricky process of gradation.

'Well, if I was right, all this build-up could have only one object: the deliberate murder of Morningside for some powerful and perfectly logical motive which was to be concealed by the impression of lunacy. But here I ran straight into what looks like a brick wall. The Coroner said a thing which came back to me very forcibly. He said that the appropriate verdict was murder if some person had deliberately placed the box on the top of the door with the intention or in the hope of killing or injuring Morningside — "even if that person could not have been absolutely certain of causing Morningside's death". That's the point, Sally. It looks as if he couldn't have been certain. And yet, if this whole elaborate plot was designed with the sole object of killing Morningside, his actual death can't have been left to chance.'

'But it was a very good chance, wasn't it? If—' Sally stopped suddenly, remembering Johnny's experiment with the Penguin.

'No,' he said. 'On the face of it, I don't think it was, and I'm not sure how far the Coroner realised that. There are, generally speaking, two different ways of approaching a door which you're going to open — or push open, if it's ajar. If you're a shy, ill-assured person, you sidle up to it — as Silcutt does — and you don't open it or push it open until you're close against it. So you're quite likely to get anything that's on top of it on your head. More likely, of course, with a box of negs than with a Penguin book, because the box is a good deal bigger, but still not certain. Or, at least, the blow is not certain to be fatal. If, on the other hand, you're fairly self-confident, as Morningside was, you extend your arm as you approach, open the door, and get what's coming to you on the forearm. If it's a box of negs it will no doubt break your arm, but it won't kill you. Either way, from the point of view of a determined murderer, it's just not good enough.'

Sally forced her mind back. 'I'm trying to remember how he was lying,' she said. 'His head and shoulders were inside the door and the rest of him outside. His right arm was stretched out ahead of him with that one negative in his hand. He—'

She stopped again, because Johnny's face had changed.

'Yes,' he said almost sharply. 'That one negative. I wondered about it at the time, and then I forgot it. How did it get there? Miss Quimper doesn't seem to have noticed it when she met him in Cuts. It's possible he had it in his pocket then, but if so, why did he take it out before he got into his office? Admittedly he was in a slightly abnormal nervous condition, and he might have made a restless movement of that kind. But—'

He got up suddenly and fetched the thick green Penguin, which he had stuck into its cover. Then he went back to Sally's desk and found a postcard.

'I think we must do this,' he said, moving a chair towards the door. 'You remember how to balance the thing?' He placed the book against the lintel in the same way as before. Then he gave it to Sally and opened the door. He laid the postcard carefully on the red mat outside, close to its inner edge, and drew the door to behind him.

Sally climbed on to the chair, placed the book, climbed down again, moved the chair, and said, 'Right.'

Johnny approached briskly. Then he stopped. A moment later the door opened, not very far. The book struck him square on the head. He was squatting just short of the mat, with the card in his hand.

He straightened up and said, 'Again, if you don't mind.'

They did it again, and this time he bent down to the card. They did it a third time, and he knelt on one knee. Every time the book fell on his head, or at least grazed it.

'This is the answer, isn't it?' said Sally at last. 'The card's the negative, I take it.'

'The card's the negative, yes. Laid just outside the door, for Morningside to pick up. He'd be bound to pick it up, and however he got down to it, the movement would bring his head into the right position, and a thing as big as the box would be almost bound to score a direct hit. The lights at that end of Peex were on, so he'd see the neg. The light in his office was off, so even if he looked up, he'd be unlikely to see the box.'

'Well done, darling,' said Sally quietly.

'Yes,' said Johnny, 'but that's not the answer, you know. Again, please.'

This time he straightened up before opening the door, and the book caught him on the forearm again. When he rose a little more slowly it just touched his forehead. At the third attempt he sidled close, and it got him on the head.

'You see?' he said. 'Come outside and I'll show you.' She followed him on to the landing, and he went on, suiting his actions to his words, 'When you squat — or stoop — or kneel — to the neg, you don't normally touch the door. Your head is closer to it than any other part of you, and I suppose it's a natural instinct not to run your head into things. I pushed the door deliberately with my hand when I was down — so — and that isn't a natural movement. The natural thing to do is to straighten up first — so — and there you are half a pace back from the door and faced with the original problem all over again. If you sidle — as Morningside almost certainly wouldn't — you'll probably get the thing on your head. If you open the door at arm's length, you certainly won't.'

'Supposing,' said Sally, as they went back into the room, 'the murderer didn't work this out quite so far. After all, he almost certainly had to do it without someone on the other side of the door to help him. Supposing he thought that with the neg the thing was foolproof. And supposing Morningside just happened to make an unnatural movement.'

Johnny shook his head. 'I don't believe it,' he said. 'I mean I don't believe that the murderer didn't work this thing out at least as carefully as we've done. Anyhow, I haven't the slightest doubt we're right about the negative, and to my mind the negative proves that the whole thing was entirely deliberate and logical.'

He found a pipe and began to fill it.

'The same question arises in Miss Quimper's case,' he said. 'Toby raised it this morning. How could her murderer be sure she'd die of a twenty-foot fall?'

'He couldn't. Unless — unless he went down after her?'

'I don't think so. It would be quite a tricky climb in the dark; he might be seen, and if he completed the work of the fall, he might well leave traces that the doctors could read. He could hardly hope to pass it off as an accident, of course; It would be far too much of a coincidence, coming so soon after Morningside's death, and you would certainly give evidence of the telephone conversation. But he may have hoped to make it look like another insane practical joke, inspired by hatred rather than by logical fear — after all, there was on the face of it nothing very much for him to fear in Miss Quimper's story. A practical joke which might prove fatal, but which couldn't be counted on to kill. Only I don't think it was a practical joke, and I think it was certain to kill.'

Sally looked anxiously at him, and he said quietly, 'I don't think she fell twenty feet. I think she fell more like eighty.'

'Do you mean she was pushed — thrown — out of the window of Toby's office?'

'I'm almost sure of it. There's no evidence that she left the building. She didn't leave by the Fleet Street entrance, and Laxton seems to think he'd have seen her if she'd gone through Garrick Square. And there were marks on Toby's window-sill this morning. That doesn't mean much, although they were fairly fresh; it's a very low sill, and people automatically put a foot on it. But there was a fresh scrape on the parapet outside, too. It's a very low parapet, and it wouldn't be frightfully difficult to tip her over. She was very small and light. The path below is very narrow, and the rail is so rotten it would be bound to break even under her weight.'

'You don't think the doctors could tell that she'd fallen eighty feet and not twenty?'

'I think they probably could. The impact and therefore the damage would be a good deal greater. But the murderer might have hoped they couldn't. He doesn't necessarily know much about the effects of falls. And remember, Sally, it was all quite impromptu, as far as we know. He had to work it out while she was talking to you. Then he walked into Toby's office, and perhaps he made some excuse to get her to lean out of the window. Or perhaps, if he was strong enough, he just made some excuse to open it, and picked her up and threw her out.'

'She'd cry out,' said Sally. 'And there must have been plenty of *Echo* people in the offices on that side of the building.'

Johnny, the ex-Commando, said without emphasis,

'Oh, there are plenty of tricks to silence someone for a few minutes.'

Sally controlled her imagination with some difficulty. 'And you think there's the same — the same pattern in Morningside's case?'

'I think there must be, if only one could see it.' Johnny was frowning. 'There's another point, you know. As you say, we've assumed all along that the trap was rigged during the canteen period. If Selina is telling the truth, I think we were meant to assume it. And that again makes the whole thing more deliberate and more subtle than we thought. It probably means that the murderer has an alibi for the canteen period and none for the time during which Morningside was in Cuts...'

His voice trailed off. Sally realised that another penny was dropping and said nothing.

After a moment he went back to the door. He opened it three or four inches, swung a solid armchair into place behind it, kicked off his slippers, and stepped on to the seat. From this position he was able to look down on the top of the door. He put a hand on it and moved it an inch or two to and fro. Sally, looking up, saw him frowning again.

Suddenly he got down, picked up the postcard from the table where he had left it, and laid it again on the mat outside. He said quickly, 'May I have the mirror out of your bag, darling?'

Sally thought she understood. She found her bag, fished out her mirror, and gave it to him.

'Turn out the lamps, will you?' he said.

In the half-darkness, with only a flicker from the neglected fire and a little light coming in from the landing, he stood on the chair, towering like an enormous shadow above her, placed the Penguin, and played about with the glass, sending a flash of light across the walls and ceiling until he had found the right angle. Then he stood quite still for a moment.

'Yes,' he said. 'That's the answer, Sally. Even with the negative as bait, he couldn't be sure of killing his man unless he was there himself, to open the door as soon as Morningside got down to it. But he couldn't see when Morningside was in position unless he used the periscope method. With the door only a little way open there's no space between it and the lintel on the hinge side, and the box would get in his light on the other. But with your mirror I can see the card and most of the mat.' He got slowly down. 'Oh, of course he was there,' he said. 'We know that he removed the cutting — probably from Morningside's hand. He had to; he wasn't expecting Miss Quimper's evidence — or Selina's — and he had to make it clear that Morningside had gone straight into his office after coming up from the canteen. If we once began to doubt that, we should see that the canteen period might not be the crucial one.' Johnny paused. 'He was clever enough to leave by the glass hatch, though; there were marks on the frame and the wall. He wouldn't want to risk disturbing the body and the negs, and he almost certainly realised that we'd expect to find marks on the hatch. Scrapes, I mean, not fingerprints; he obviously wore gloves.'

Sally said slowly, 'And still almost no one has an alibi. Teddy could have come back by the coal-hole; on the new reckoning he'd have had plenty of time. Michael Knox could have come back during Laxton's patrol and waited. So could Silcutt.'

Johnny said, 'Darling, don't you understand? We were meant to assume that the trap was rigged during the canteen period. That ought to mean that the murderer has an alibi for the canteen period.'

'No,' she said almost violently. 'No, Johnny. Not—'

The telephone rang, sharp and nerve-racking in the

darkness. Sally jumped. Johnny turned on the light at the door, strode over to the fireplace, and picked up the receiver.

'Hullo,' he said, and then, 'Good evening, Toby.'

Sally moved over to him and, half-reluctantly, sat down on the arm of his chair and began to listen.

'Any news your end?' asked Toby.

Johnny told him the Longwall story, and his voice came to them in a distorted squeak of indignation. 'The man must be half-witted!'

'He's stupid,' said Johnny, 'and so pleased with himself that it never struck him his plan might go wrong. I'll let you have the prints on Monday, Toby. What you do about it is up to you, but if you don't mind, I'd like to talk to Teddy before anyone else gets going on him. If I could only wash him out as far as the murders are concerned, it would simplify matters.'

'He's all yours to start with,' said Toby a little wearily. 'Anything else?'

Sally was just aware of the pause before Johnny said, 'I don't think so.' Toby apparently wasn't. He went straight on.

'I've got something more about Michael Knox. You remember we heard he was in the Cat-in-Boots on Wednesday evening between six and half past, and perhaps later. Well, I found a man tonight who was with him there from about a quarter to seven till about ten past. So he would seem to be in the clear. The Cat is five minutes from Echo House by taxi — I tried it. He couldn't have gone back and rigged the trap and returned to the Cat between six-thirty and six-forty-five, and he couldn't have gone back and rigged the trap between seven-ten and seven-twenty. Five minutes would be enough for the actual rigging, no doubt, but not for getting in unobserved by the coal-hole and getting upstairs as well.'

'No,' said Johnny.

'And I've got some idea why he wouldn't say where he'd been. Not that that matters now.'

'I'd be quite interested to hear it, all the same.'

'Very well, but stop me if it bores you. The man I met tonight is on the *Echo* — *Daily*, not *Sunday*. His name is Wilson, and he was actually looking for Michael on Wednesday evening. He'd heard a buzz that afternoon that the IRA was planning a raid on a certain Army camp on Salisbury Plain, and that the police had got hold of it and would be there in force. As a matter of fact the buzz was partially true; you probably heard about the raid. The police evidently didn't know about it in advance, but it wasn't a very impressive affair anyway.'

'I remember,' said Johnny. 'Half a dozen masked men; some binding and gagging and a little wild shooting, and only half a dozen rifles gone at the end of it. No arrests.'

'That's right. Well, Wilson wasn't sure how likely the buzz was to be true, and Mike was a rather obvious person to ask. He's a Fleet Street man, with a magnificent nose for news, and at the moment he doesn't represent any rival concern. He's an Irishman and knows a lot of other Irishmen. And there was one particular point. He's got a young Irish cousin called Terence Dowd. I'd heard of him as the author of that so-called realist novel *Fair City*. I never know,' said Toby parenthetically, 'whether the Irish at home are really like that or not. But I didn't know until tonight that the boy was a relation of Mike's. He's not in Fleet Street. But some weeks ago Mike made an unsuccessful attempt to get him on to the *Reflector* — I believe that was the occasion of Mike's row with his editor — and Dowd was about the place for a couple of days. Wilson met him in some pub with Mike and was mildly interested in him because he dropped mysterious and sinister hints about being in the IRA.

'But Mike said he'd heard no buzz about a raid. When Wilson mentioned Dowd and his alleged political connections, Mike looked down his nose and said the child had a vivid imagination. In any case, he — the child — had gone back to Ireland. But five minutes later, to Wilson's surprise, Mike murmured something about a date, and slipped away. Wilson's a suspicious type — we're apt to get like that in Fleet Street — and he at once wondered if, after all, Mike was representing someone or doing freelance work. If so, he might have decided to go down to the camp himself and try for the story. Wilson mulled it over, and then went back to Echo House to see if they'd heard any more about the buzz. They hadn't, and he was sent off on something more certain, if less exciting. In fact, I was there when he went off, though he didn't mention then that he'd been with Mike. I was gossiping with someone on the *Echo* just before I met you at eight.' Toby drew breath.

'I think it's quite possible,' he said, 'that Mike went down to Wiltshire. It's conceivable that he got involved in the raid for the sake of the story — he's entirely reckless. In that case he might be extremely reluctant to tell the police what he'd been doing. No doubt he'd be prepared to admit it in the last resort, but it would be quite understandable if he tried to get away with it. Wilson alone gives him an alibi, of course, but if Wilson gave any account of their conversation the police might well guess where Mike had gone after it. Or they might make trouble for Dowd. He's presumably safe for the moment, but he may want to come back to England one day.'

'Yes,' said Johnny. 'You haven't seen any report of the raid which might be Knox's?'

'No. I know his work well, and I'm quite sure there

hasn't been one. But Mike has high standards — professionally speaking — and the raid was a bit of a washout. If he didn't feel he could do himself justice he mightn't have written anything, or he mightn't have turned it in. Or he might have destroyed it after Morningside's death, feeling that it wasn't quite the sort of alibi he would wish to have. If it was written for a Sunday paper, that is. If it was for a daily, it would have had to be turned in before he heard about the murder.'

'Yes. Well, that's very interesting, Toby. It gives one food for thought. I shall see you on Monday morning. May I have Teddy about eleven?'

'Certainly. I'll see he's in then. Goodnight, Johnny.'

'Goodnight,' said Johnny, and put down the receiver.

'Wilson doesn't give Michael an alibi, of course,' said Sally. 'Not according to the revised version. Toby would know that if — if—'

'Yes, he would,' said Johnny shortly. 'But he'd have to assume we didn't.'

Sally changed the subject. 'Supposing Michael's guilty, why didn't he give us his alibi for the canteen period?'

'Well, even so it might be a little tricky, because of the IRA aspect. He'd have gone to the Cat-in-Boots, where presumably he was likely to find someone who knew him, in order to establish an alibi, but not a slightly compromising one. But I don't think that's really a good enough reason for concealing it — from us, at any rate. I wonder if he didn't see possibilities in the IRA aspect and turn it to his advantage. Perhaps he deliberately left Wilson with the impression that he was going down to Wiltshire. Later, he becomes mysterious about his movements, and leaves it to someone else to find Wilson. If it's only a question of the canteen period, Wilson clears him, whatever interpretation the police may put on his reticence. If he's pressed about the post-canteen period — the Cuts period — he can very reluctantly produce a rather discreditable account of the raid, which will make it fairly clear that he hadn't time to go back to Echo House first, and everyone will say that he really wouldn't have told such a damaging story if it hadn't been true.'

'Excellent,' said Sally. 'But where has he got his story?'

'He's used to going and getting stories. Some soldier at the camp, perhaps. Or possibly Terence Dowd hasn't gone back to Ireland after all. Anyhow, Knox would have known, as everyone else seems to have done, that Morningside nearly always worked late on Wednesdays and had supper in the canteen. He'd have known that they start serving supper at a quarter to seven. He could have been back at Echo House at a quarter past and waited somewhere. If Morningside hadn't gone into Cuts, he could have found some way of getting him out of Peex for a few minutes.'

'Yes,' said Sally. 'It's good enough.'

'He hated Morningside,' said Johnny. 'Morningside stood for everything he dislikes most — middle-class morality, narrowness, stupidity, intolerance. Morningside stood between him and Selina — or so he seems to have thought. Morningside broke up young Dowd's love-affair, and to some extent his career. Knox may even have taken this job in order to avenge Dowd's wrongs. After all, he lost his last job for the boy's sake.'

'Morningside thought he had been writing the letters,' said Sally. 'At least, that seemed to be his final decision.'

'So it did. Of all our suspects, Sally, Knox has the best brain, and he's not hampered by normal scruples. And he's got an alibi for the canteen period, though he won't admit it. I've no right to say it, but I think he's going to be our man.'

CHAPTER ELEVEN

Sunday morning was damp and depressing. A yellow fog hung over St Cross Square in shreds and patches. The leafless trees in the square garden dripped steadily on to the drab winter grass and the wet tarmac, and the sound of traffic, thin today in any case and never very noticeable here, was blotted out in an all-absorbent silence.

They hadn't had much time to read the news yesterday, and Johnny went out to buy Sunday papers of the type they didn't usually take. Miss Quimper's death had given the Press a fresh fillip. The *Sunday Echo* was having the time of its life. But no one seemed to realise that Miss Quimper had fallen from a sixth-floor window, and not from the narrow path above the bombed site — no one except, almost certainly, the police.

Just before eleven o'clock Sally and Johnny went across the square to St Cross Church — an elegant little Regency survival which had somehow been saved from the improvements of the Victorian age. This morning it was almost dark. The fog-veils dimmed the lights and hung in front of the stained glass and the curved grey walls with their memorial tablets. Several members of the choir seemed to have lost their voices, and the

Vicar, who was a noted preacher, had a bad cold. But Sally had to admit that even if he had been at his best her attention would probably have wandered. She couldn't help thinking about the Archives: about Morningside and Miss Quimper, who were dead; about Toby and Selina and Teddy and Michael Knox, whom Johnny believed to be a murderer. She was glad when the service was over and they came out into the thick, damp air and crossed the square to their house. Peter was up at the nursery window, waving to them, and they waved back.

It was Nanny's Sunday afternoon off, and though she said she didn't want it in this weather, they took the children off her hands after lunch, and played primitive games in the drawing room till tea-time.

After tea Johnny looked something up in the Telephone Directory, and then said casually to Sally, 'I'm going to look in on Michael Knox.'

Before she could answer Peter asked inevitably, 'Who's Michael Knox?'

'He's an Irish friend of mine,' said Johnny.

'Where does he live?'

'In Crawley Street. Just round the corner.'

'Can I come too, Daddy?'

'No,' said Johnny simply. It was never any good being diplomatic with Peter.

'Will you be back in time to tell me an Albert story?'

'I won't promise, but I expect so. I shouldn't think I shall be more than three-quarters of an hour.'

'All right. If you'll try very hard, Daddy—'

'I'll do my best. Goodbye.'

If Sally had had an opportunity of arguing she would probably have done it. But she told herself it was silly to worry. Michael Knox was a powerful man, but he was unlikely to be a match for Johnny's strength and Johnny's Commando tricks.

Johnny walked into the drawing room again a quarter of an hour later. Peter looked up and said, 'Hullo, Daddy. Have you seen Michael Knox?'

'No,' said Johnny. 'He was out.'

'Good,' said Peter brightly. 'Now we can have the Albert story, can't we?'

In due course Nanny collected first the twins and then Peter. She said she might as well be putting them to bed as sitting knitting, and Sally was grateful. It was after peace had descended on the drawing room that Johnny said, 'Funny thing. No one answered Knox's bell, but two of his windows were lighted.'

'Perhaps he's careless about lights,' said Sally.

'Perhaps he is. The simple explanation is usually the right one.'

'Johnny, are you going back?'

'Oh, yes,' said Johnny. 'I must see him.' He looked at her. 'Don't be silly, darling. There's nothing to worry about. I think I'd better go now.'

'Can't I come with you?'

'No,' said Johnny simply.

But again he was back in a quarter of an hour.

'Still out, apparently,' he said. 'I shall have to try again after supper. I don't want to ring up first; I'd rather he wasn't expecting me.'

He went out again at eight, and this time he didn't come back. The French carriage clock on the drawing room mantelpiece struck the half-hour, and then nine o'clock. By that time Sally was really anxious. Crawley Street was less than five minutes' walk from St Cross Square.

It would be idiotic to go to the police as soon as this. She wanted to go straight round to Crawley Street and ring Michael Knox's bell, but if this delay meant that Johnny had at last persuaded him to talk, an interruption might spoil everything.

But at a quarter past nine she couldn't wait any longer. She put on her old tweed coat and tied a scarf over her head. She didn't want a muddle, so she scribbled a note to Johnny on the telephone pad in the drawing room, folded it, and propped it up against the carriage clock. Then she checked Michael Knox's address in the Telephone Directory, and ran downstairs, half believing she would find Johnny on the doorstep.

But only the fog came in. It was cold and raw, but still patchy, and she could see the misty streetlamps, the shining pavements, the dark shapes of the trees in the garden. She turned to the right and hurried.

The first turning was Sedley Street. Halfway down it she turned left into Crawley Street. She wasn't necessarily going to interrupt; she would walk past the house and see what she could. She wanted Fifteen, but in the dark the numbers were difficult to read, and it was only after she had passed half a dozen houses that she realised she was on the even side. She turned to cross the street and was halfway over when she saw the right number silhouetted on a fanlight against a lighted hall.

Knox had said the top flat. She looked up and saw chinks of light round two of the three windows. As she looked, they vanished.

Her immediate reaction was relief. The interview was over, and Knox was seeing Johnny downstairs. Then she was suddenly afraid again. In that case, would he bother to turn off the light? Unless he was going out himself — She stepped back. She must be near enough to recognise whoever was going to be silhouetted against the light in the hall, and not near enough to be recognised.

Perhaps thirty seconds passed. Then the front door swung open and Michael Knox shot out and down the steps. The light from the hall shone on his blue-black hair.

Johnny came after him. He swung to the left, with a hand on the railing, and Johnny swung too. They ran hard along the damp pavement, their footsteps sounding flat and dull in the thick air. They passed Sally without noticing her, and then Knox turned and cut across to the mouth of Sedley Street, and Johnny followed. As soon as they were round the corner the sound of their feet died.

It was extraordinarily eerie, and almost unreal, partly, perhaps, because of its quietness. Neither of the men had spoken, far less cried out. It might have been a scene from a silent film. Sally, a little dazed, was turning the way they had gone when a voice with a brogue like clotted cream said, 'Good evening, Mrs Heldar. You look like a girl out of Hans Andersen with the fog-crystals in your hair. And what's your husband after?'

For a moment she was rigid with fear. Then she put up her hands automatically to pull her scarf forward, and said, 'He went to see you.'

'I'm sorry I wasn't in, then. I'm just back now.'

'Who is it that he's chasing?' asked Sally. She tried so hard to keep the bewilderment out of her voice that it sounded flat and stupid.

'Indeed, I don't know,' said Knox. 'I didn't see. Let's walk on the way they went, shall we? I don't suppose we shall catch them up, but it's your way home, isn't it?'

She was thankful he hadn't asked her to come up to his flat. But to walk with him through the foggy darkness and the thick silence was almost as bad. She was sure he had lied to her. She hadn't heard him approach — he walked almost soundlessly on what must be rubber soles — but she was sure he did know the man Johnny was chasing and had seen him.

'A dirty night,' he said blandly, as they turned into Sedley Street. 'Mind, now; the pavements are slippery.'

He took her arm, felt her slight movement, and let her go. 'All right. But for your information, I am not a murderer.'

She managed to say calmly, 'I hope not.'

He laughed a little, and they walked quickly on up the street. They were fifty yards from the square when she heard a car coming round it from the right. At the same moment Johnny shouted. Then a figure shot out from the left-hand corner and showed black against the car's lights as they swung into sight. There was a scream of brakes, and Michael Knox went forward like an arrow.

Then someone started swearing. It sounded like a taxi-driver. The language was hair-raising, but it was perfectly clear that no one was hurt. Sally, running after Knox, who had slowed down, heard someone attempt to answer, and get cursed again, more mildly this time.

'Bloody young fool, runnin' straight across me bows—'

Johnny was there, holding a tall young man by one arm.

'All right,' he said. 'It was my young friend's fault. I'll tell him off. He's not used to London traffic yet.'

'You're tellin' me, sir. You keep an eye on 'im, for Gawd's sake. 'E's not safe aht.' But Johnny's manner was having its usual effect. 'Take yer anywhere, sir?'

'No, thanks. We're only a few doors from home.'

'Right you are, sir. I'll be on my way, then.'

Knox took a step forward. Perhaps he had an idea of getting the young man away in the taxi. But before he could speak a policeman came running round the corner, his cape glistening with the fog.

'What's happened here?' he asked. 'Anyone hurt? Oh, it's you, Mr Heldar.'

Johnny explained briefly, exonerating the driver, making very little of the incident. The policeman was satisfied. This was his beat, and he knew the Heldars well. The taxi moved on down Sedley Street, and he said goodnight to them and walked on round the square. He seemed to have taken Knox for the nucleus of the inevitable crowd which gathers round any sort of accident.

Johnny was silent for a moment, and Sally intervened. She was determined not to leave him alone with these men, and she knew he was trying to decide how best to get rid of her.

She turned to Knox. 'I think you'd better come along with us,' she said. 'You and your cousin. Then we can talk things over.'

The boy started violently, but Johnny held him. Knox hesitated for a moment. Then he smiled and bowed.

'We shall be delighted to accept your invitation,' he said. 'Come along, Terence. Don't be a fool, boy. If you run away again, Heldar will go to the police. If we explain things to him nicely, there's just a chance he won't.'

The boy said nothing, but Sally saw his eyes gleaming in the light of a streetlamp as they walked on.

In the hall she could see him properly for the first time. Twenty years ago, she thought, Knox had probably looked just like this. Terence Dowd was nearly as tall as he was; not quite so thin, but not yet arrived at his full strength, and moving with an awkward grace which on the stage would have been extraordinarily impressive, for there was about it the suggestion of half-controlled violence seen in a wild animal. A caged animal, thought Sally. The narrow, high-boned face under the shining blue-black hair was very handsome and very young. Knox's long, expressive mouth was there, sensitive and sulky, and the sapphire eyes were hot. The boy wore crumpled grey flannel trousers and a navy-blue fisherman's jersey.

Sally took the guests upstairs while Johnny went to collect drinks. She had only just handed round the cigarette-box when he came in with the tray. Both the Irishmen took their whisky neat. Johnny looked at her, and without consulting her gave her whisky too, with a good deal of soda. Then he helped himself and sat down.

'I'll start, if I may, Knox,' he said. 'I tried to call on you twice between tea and supper. The door of the house was unlocked. I got no answer when I rang at your door upstairs, but I noticed on both occasions that two of your windows were lighted.'

'Dolt,' said Knox amiably to his cousin. The boy's mouth twisted just as Sally had seen Knox's do.

'I got there for the third time,' continued Johnny, 'just after eight. Still no answer, and still the lighted windows. I don't suppose I'd have waited, even then, but on my way down I met a woman who I think must be one of your Belgian neighbours. She opened her door and peeped out, and I asked her if she knew when you would be in. She said she didn't, but she looked so worried that I began to wonder. I went downstairs, and I'm afraid I cheated her. I opened the front door and shut it again — loudly. After that I heard her door close.

'I thought something was going on — something, please observe, which might concern me, indirectly at least, as representing the National Press Archives. So I waited in the hall. I waited till about twenty past nine, and then I heard your door open and shut. I looked up the staircase well and saw your cousin coming down. I thought it was you at first.'

'Dolt again,' said Knox.

'I wanted cigarettes,' said the boy sulkily, speaking almost for the first time. His accent was slight — a little more marked than Knox's when Knox wasn't being de-liberately Irish, and quite fascinating.

Johnny went on. 'When he reached the hall, I saw he wasn't you, and I accosted him. I asked him if he wasn't Terence Dowd. It was a guess, of course, but it seemed to me a fairly safe one. And he immediately confirmed it by taking to his heels.'

This time Knox merely sighed.

'I'm not as young as he is,' said Johnny, 'and I shouldn't have caught him without the taxi. He led me up Sedley Street and round the square — I know the ground a little better than he does, so I managed to keep my place. Then he ran in front of the taxi, and I caught up, and the rest you know. But I don't quite understand how you and my wife got there.'

'I walked round to pick you up,' said Sally. 'I was just crossing Crawley Street to Mr Knox's front door when you came out.'

'I see.' Sally knew that he did see, and that she hadn't heard the last of it. But he let it go for the moment and turned back to Knox. 'If you like to deny my right to ask questions, I can't really press the point. But what you said yourself a little while ago is perfectly true. If you run out on me again, I must go to the police.'

'That's obvious to me,' said Knox. 'Terence will see it tomorrow or the next day. All right. Go ahead.'

'On Wednesday evening,' said Johnny, 'you were in the Cat-in-Boots, talking to a man called Wilson, of the *Daily Echo*. He asked you if you'd heard a buzz about an IRA raid arranged for that night. You said you hadn't. Was that true?'

'Yes.'

'But I think you believed the buzz when he told you about it. Had Dowd let something slip?'

'He hadn't said in so many words that he was going on a raid. But he'd been behaving like a stage conspirator for the last fortnight or so. Reticences and mysteries. Unexplained telephone calls and visits to pubs. I was fairly certain he wasn't in with the IRA, and it transpired later on that I was right. His crowd is just playing at soldiers. But I knew he was in with something fairly Republican, and my news instinct is highly developed. So when Wilson mentioned the buzz, I put two and two together.'

The boy's face was stormy. But Knox paid no attention to him.

'And what did you do after that?' asked Johnny.

'I took a taxi to a couple of pubs where I thought Terence might be. I was pretty sure that even if he hadn't started for the camp, I wouldn't find him at home; he knew I disapproved of his activities, and he'd have made a point of being out of the way before I got back, in case I asked him where he was going. But I didn't find him, so I went on to the flat, just on the chance. He wasn't there, and I asked the Lemaires, down below, if they'd seen or heard him go out. Marthe said yes, she'd heard him go downstairs a little after five. I didn't suppose he'd started for Wiltshire at five; the raid would be fixed for the small hours, so I knew I had time. I got out my car — I keep it just round the corner — and went off. As you may have heard, Wilson's buzz said that the police had got wind of the proceedings and would be there in considerable force, and I was quite sure Terence and his friends were not sufficiently experienced to avoid arrest if they did turn up.

'I had a hell of a journey. It was drizzling when I left London, but farther west it had been raining heavily, and somewhere in the wilds of Hampshire I ran into deep water. I got out of it on the starter, and of course my engine was flooded. She's an old car, and she hasn't got baffle-plates. It took me nearly two hours to dry her out.

'I got to the neighbourhood of the camp about one o'clock. By that time it was pouring again, and I spent a good half-hour looking for the place. When I'd found it, I parked the car in among some bushes and started going round the wire. I couldn't find the car Terence and Co were presumably using, but after a little I found a place where the wire had been cut. I was on my way in when I heard a couple of shots and some shouting. Then people started running towards me. I slipped out again and waited. Half a dozen conspirators in masks and mackintoshes came out, and Terence was the last of them. So I grabbed him and ran him back to my car. He'd got a nice new rifle, but I made him leave it behind; I don't like incontrovertible evidence. His colleagues scattered and got away, and we drove home by ourselves. He's been lying low ever since, because his mask came off during a short battle in the guardroom. Also he was seen hanging about the camp last Sunday, when they did a reconnaissance. So I thought we'd better play for safety, at any rate until the Archives affair is cleared up. I'd have sent him home, but the Irish boats and planes were bound to be watched. And he's never hidden his light under a bushel. Dozens of people know his politics.'

Sally nodded. No one who had once seen Terence Dowd could fail to know him again, and he wouldn't be hard to describe.

'Who told you about Terence?' asked Knox suddenly. 'Camberley?'

'No,' said Johnny. 'Does he know?'

'Some of it. But I didn't really think he was responsible. He might have thought it his duty to tell you, but he'd probably have told me he was going to. He has a strong British sense of fair play. So I don't suppose he told the police about Terence either.'

'I shouldn't think so.'

'All right. I'll restrain my natural curiosity. But Lindesay called on us, as perhaps you don't know. Late yesterday afternoon. Terence went down the fire-escape to the Lemaires — he always does if someone calls while I'm in — and I entertained the Inspector. It was safe enough; there are no outward and visible signs of Terence's occupation. I'm rather particular about that. By the way, did you hear the full story as given to the police?'

'I believe so,' said Johnny. 'Now, what I am interested in is the names of the pubs where you looked for Dowd on Wednesday evening.'

'"Oh Sammy, Sammy, vy worn't there a alleybi? If your governor don't prove a alleybi, he'll be what the Italians call reg'larly flummoxed." The first pub was the Territorial Arms, in Apostle Street, off the Strand, and the second was the Three Sisters in Woolpack Street. Both perfectly respectable houses. And, of course, you'll want to see the Lemaires. I've already told you they're hopeless liars, but by all means talk to them. Come back with us now, if you like — that is, if you've finished with us.'

'I don't think I've anything more to ask you. I will come with you, if I may.'

Knox stood up, smiling. 'Thank you for your hospitality, Mrs Heldar,' he said. 'I hope we shall meet again when you don't suspect me of murder.'

Before Sally could find a suitable reply, Terence Dowd said in his sullen, silken voice, 'It's very good of you to receive a hunted man.'

'He's been reading Sean O'Casey,' said Knox a little wearily. 'Goodnight, Mrs Heldar.'

Twenty minutes later Johnny reappeared.

'Daniel out of the lions' den,' he said. 'Don't look so ridiculously relieved.'

'Sorry.'

Johnny sat down beside her and kissed her. Then he said, "The Lemaires swear that Knox looked in on them about ten to eight on Wednesday evening. They add that he was looking for Dowd, and Madame says she saw his car go past the house five minutes later — though I'm afraid that's a flight of her imagination. I went to see them as a matter of form; they're obviously unreliable, and Knox has had every opportunity of briefing them. But even if they're telling the truth, he could at a pinch have killed Morningside and got to them by seven-fifty. It would have meant a taxi, of course. But the pubs are the important places, and they're closed now.'

After a moment Sally asked, 'Do you think Terence is his cousin?'

'I wondered that too,' said Johnny. 'The resemblance is extraordinary. Knox must be in his early forties, and the boy in his early twenties. I wouldn't be surprised. It would explain why Knox took the Archives job, and why he hasn't been seen about so much in Fleet Street lately. He'd want more time with the boy.'

'He covered up for him to the last possible moment.' Sally repeated her conversation with Knox. 'And when he thought Terence had been run over, he ran like a hare.'

Johnny nodded. 'And it would make his motive ten or twenty times stronger. I think I said last night, Sally, that if he were pressed about the Cuts period, he would produce a rather discreditable account of the raid, which would make it fairly clear that he hadn't had time to go back to Echo House before he started. And that is precisely what he's done.'

CHAPTER TWELVE

Johnny was late for lunch on Monday. Sally, whom he had warned, fed Nanny and the children and had them upstairs again by the time he came in. He looked a little discouraged, and she let him eat before she asked any questions. When they had finished, he lit cigarettes for them both and put his elbows on the table.

'I talked to Teddy,' he said. 'When I confronted him with the Longwall story, he got frightened — really frightened — and admitted the whole thing. He also admitted that Morningside had discovered part of the truth and threatened to report him. But he swore — several times over — that after he'd left Longwall on Wednesday evening, he went straight to the Alcazar, and didn't leave it again until about nine-thirty. He saw the last part of *Mothers' Day* — his original story, you remember, was that it had sent him to sleep — some advertisements, and the whole of *Injun Trail*. He swore, again, that on Friday evening, when he'd left his photographic buddy, he went to Holborn and tried to see a girlfriend of his who lives somewhere near Gamage's. But she was out — the whole household was out — so he went home, arriving there about half past seven.

From that time on his aunt and uncle give him an alibi, which of course is no use to him or anyone else.' Johnny sighed.

'I'm inclined to believe him,' he said. 'I think that in some ways he's a good kid. But he lied when he first told his story, and look at his record!'

'I know,' said Sally.

They contemplated Teddy's record for a minute or two in gloomy silence. Then Johnny said, 'On the other hand, there's Knox. I've been to his pubs. The proprietor of the Territorial Arms says he came in on Wednesday evening sometime between a quarter past seven and half past; the barmaid of the Three Sisters says he came in on Wednesday evening between half past seven and twenty-five to eight. Both witnesses remember him, because he asked if they had seen Dowd, whom they know, and because he was so like Dowd. The barmaid remembers the time of his visit almost exactly because Dowd had in fact been in the Three Sisters with a friend between half past six and seven, and she looked at the clock so that she could tell Knox how long ago he had left. She says she had never seen Knox before — though I gathered she would have no objection to seeing him again — and the proprietor of the Territorial Arms says he sees him only very occasionally. That's probably true; both the pubs are a bit off his usual beat. And neither of the witnesses appears to be a compatriot of his. So I don't think they're lying for him.'

'So there is "a alleybi".'

'It would seem so. If he was in the Three Sisters between half past seven and twenty-five to eight, that clears him completely according to the revised version. If he was in the Territorial Arms before that and after he left the Cat-in-Boots at ten past seven, that clinches it. He can't have got to the Territorial Arms much before twenty past, and he must have gone straight on from there to the Three Sisters; it's another ten minutes' drive.'

Johnny stubbed out his cigarette and pushed back his chair. 'I'm going back to the Archives,' he said. 'I rather want to see Camberley, and Toby thought he might be in this afternoon.'

'Why Camberley?'

'Well, I'd rather like to try Teddy on him. If Teddy's telling the truth, Camberley won't get any more out of him than I have, but he's the best judge of men I've ever met, and I'd like his opinion.'

'I see. Are you — are you going to talk to him about Toby, too?'

'Darling, I've got to. Now that we think the murderer deliberately created an alibi for the canteen period — and now that Knox seems to be out of it — I've got to consider Toby.'

After a moment Sally said, 'I'd like to come with you, then.'

'Do you mean that? It won't be very enjoyable.'

Sally hadn't meant quite that. She had recognised in Johnny the particular symptoms of anxiety which meant that he had begun seriously to suspect someone whom he really liked. She didn't want to leave him to investigate Toby alone. If he were going to make any disturbing discovery, she didn't want him to make it alone, and as likely as not keep it from her and worry about it by himself.

'I'd rather be there,' she said.

* * *

THE ECHO's young men were apparently as wide awake as ever, and the Heldars used the side door, and approached it from the back of the building. They were

crossing Garrick Square when Michael Knox, re-
turning late from lunch, strode into it from a narrow
passage on the east side.

'Good afternoon to you,' he said, and raised two
long fingers to his temple in a casual salute.

'Good afternoon,' said Johnny. 'I'm glad to see you.
I've been doing a pub-crawl — hobnobbing with barmaids and such — and as far as I can see I needn't
bother Lindesay.'

Sally thought she saw relief in Knox's eyes, but it
was generally difficult to read them.

'Thank you very much,' he said.

'You're very welcome,' said Sally on an impulse.

'Thank you. I appreciate that.'

They went in, past Laxton's opposite number at his
desk, down the steps and along the passage. One of the
girls from Negs followed them into the lift, and it was
impossible to say any more. But as they went up Sally
caught Knox's eye, and his long mouth curled. There
was cynicism in the smile, but there was something
warmer too. She had to smile back.

When they came out into the back passage Knox
gave the Heldars a jerk of his long head and turned towards Cuts. They followed Miss Quimper's girl into
Peex and went on to the farther end. Johnny glanced
round, and Selina materialised from behind the filing
cabinets.

'Good afternoon,' she said. 'I'm afraid Toby isn't
here; he went to lunch very late. Is there anything I can
do for you?'

'That's very kind of you,' said Johnny. 'I suppose
you've no idea if Brigadier Camberley is anywhere in
the building?'

'I'm afraid I haven't. He's not up here; I know that.
I'll get on to the *Echo* switchboard and ask them if they
can find him.'

'Thank you so much. There's no need to mention my name to the switchboard. Just ask for him, if you don't mind, and if you get him tell him I'm here. Say John or something. The *Echo* men are rather ghoulish.'

'I know,' said Selina. 'I'll do my best.'

But she couldn't find Camberley. After ten minutes on the telephone she reported that he didn't seem to be in the building, and that a usually reliable source thought he was at the House. Johnny thanked her and apologised for bothering her.

Teddy appeared suddenly, coming from the other end of the room. He was carrying a handful of glossy prints. They had evidently been in a cellophane bag, but he had taken them out and was looking at them as he came. He wandered on to the open door of the typists' office without noticing the Heldars. Selina had gone back to her work.

'Cor stone the crows!' he said. 'I wonder if they'll syndicate this stuff after all, now old Morny's gone. "Meself when Young." Look at the Cabinet Minister in a short frock and long curls! Might 'ave murdered 'im meself if I thought 'e was all set to publish one like that of me.'

Either he had recovered with rather surprising speed from his interview with Johnny, or — more likely — he was trying to conceal his apprehensions under an aggressive jauntiness.

'Pipe down, Teddy,' said Pat's voice. 'Those are from the dark-room, I suppose. Mr Morningside must have sent the negs down before he was killed. Where's the slip for them?'

'I dunno,' said Teddy with unconvincing blankness. 'Don't think they give me one.'

'Don't be silly,' said Pam's voice. 'They always give you one. Try your pockets.'

Teddy, standing just inside the door, with his back

to the Heldars, slapped his pockets with large gestures. 'Not 'ere,' he said.

'*Feel* in your pockets,' said Pat coldly.

Teddy slid two fingers into his breast pocket. 'Not 'ere,' he said again, shaking his red head. He put his hand deliberately into a side pocket.

Someone lost patience. A chair skidded back, and Pat advanced on Teddy, coming into the Heldars' field of vision. He raised his arms. 'Okay,' he said. 'You can search me.'

Pat emptied his pockets briskly, laying the contents on a side table. The breast pocket yielded an orange silk handkerchief, obviously for show only, a ballpoint pen, and a propelling pencil, and the inner breast pocket a cheap wallet hideously patterned in no known tartan. The side pockets were empty, except for fluff; evidently Teddy was afraid of spoiling the set of his jacket. From his trouser pockets Pat produced a handkerchief for use, which she dropped on the table from understandably fastidious fingers, a squashed packet of cigarettes and a cheap lighter, some loose change, two lengths of string, some rubber bands, a couple of paperclips, and finally two pieces of crumpled paper, one very small.

'Cinema ticket,' she said, and threw the scrap out of sight, presumably into a wastepaper basket. Then she unfolded the other paper. 'Yes, this is it. All right, Teddy, thank you.'

'Sendin' me away so soon?' asked Teddy languishingly.

'Yes,' said Pat. 'We've got work to do. Shut the door, please.'

Teddy's further protest was drowned by the rattle of typewriter keys. He swung round, saw Johnny, and turned slowly crimson, the colour flooding up his pale wedge of a face. Johnny nodded to him, and he swallowed convulsively and almost ran.

Johnny, who had seemed to be waiting out of idle curiosity, watched him go out by the back way and then knocked on the typists' door. They both called, 'Come in,' and he opened it.

'Good afternoon, Mr Heldar. What can we do for you?'

Johnny was drawing Sally into the room. He shut the door behind them and said quietly, 'May I see the cinema ticket you took off Teddy? In here, is it?' He squatted down beside Pam's wastepaper bin.

'The cinema ticket?' said Pam. 'Oh! He said he was at the pictures on Wednesday evening, only he couldn't prove it. Will the ticket give him an alibi, Mr Heldar?'

'I'm not sure, but I hope it may.' Johnny had found it and was looking at it carefully. 'It's got a number on it. It's the half you get back from the usherette, of course. I don't know quite how these things work, but I'll hand it over to Inspector Lindesay and he'll find out. Of course Teddy may quite well have got it some other evening.'

'I hope not, poor kid,' said Pam.

'I hope not too. Have you got an envelope I can put it in? Thank you; that's fine. You'll keep this to yourselves, won't you? If it is going to be a wash-out it would be a pity if people got to know about it.'

'We won't say anything,' said Pat. She hesitated. 'We oughtn't to be asking this, but it's not that we're curious. Oh, well, it is, of course. But it's really because it's such a strain, just waiting and wondering. Do you know who did it?'

'No,' said Johnny. 'I'm afraid I don't. I'm sorry, because I do know how you feel. We had someone murdered at our shop once, and we both know what it's like.'

'Yes,' said Sally. 'It's a frightful strain.'

'You can't believe it's anyone in the office,' said Pam.

'And yet every time you see anyone you wonder: Is it him?'

THE HELDARS STOPPED at the post office in Fleet Street, and Johnny rang up Scotland Yard and was put through to Lindesay. He explained about the cinema ticket, and Lindesay was pleased and entirely approving — its discovery, of course, had obviously not entailed any poaching on police preserves. He said he would send a man to pick it up; was Mr Heldar going back to Heldar Brothers? Johnny said he was, and after further civilities rang off. He and Sally cut through to Holborn and took the same bus to Southampton Row, and there Sally got off and walked home.

* * *

AFTER SUPPER that evening Camberley called on the Heldars. When the bell rang Sally was quite sure it was Toby. But after Johnny had gone down to the front door, she recognised the deep voice on the staircase. She relaxed, and then she remembered why Johnny had wanted to see Camberley, and wished he wasn't here.

But she almost changed her mind when he came in. He was so warm and friendly that her polite welcome became entirely sincere. They put him on the sofa and gave him a cigarette, and Johnny got him a drink.

He waited till Johnny had helped himself, and then nodded and smiled to Sally over his glass and drank. Then he said, 'What a very attractive house this is.'

'I'm glad you like it,' said Sally.

'I like it very much.' He smiled again — a slow, reminiscent smile this time. 'I was brought up in a small flat over a grocer's shop, in a little town in the West Country.' (So that, thought Sally, was the pleasant accent below the surface of his voice.) 'It was full of the worst possible Victorian and Edwardian stuff — horse-hair chairs, plush tablecloths, hideous floral wallpapers, presents from Margate, and the like. It didn't worry me when I was a child, and I didn't begin to think about furnishings for a long time after that, but during my years in the Army I gradually got ideas about peaceful rooms with things like these in them. I've done what I can with my own flat — I should like to show it to you some day — but this is the best I've seen yet.'

Sally said they would love to see his flat, and Johnny, a little to her surprise, explained how they had come by Mark Mercator's furniture. He very seldom gave explanations which involved his detective successes, and it pleased her to see him drawn out.

When he had finished, Camberley said, 'That's extraordinarily interesting — to me. I don't suppose it was so much fun for you. A detective story isn't very entertaining when you're right in the middle of it. All the same, I'd better get on with it, and tell you why I'm here. In the first place, I had a word with Lindesay a little while ago, and he says Teddy is in the clear — thanks entirely to you. The police had already made enquiries at the cinema, of course, but no one remembered the boy; it's evidently a biggish place. But when they went back with the ticket, the people there were able to say that it was issued on Wednesday evening before seven-thirty — probably not very long before. It was near the end of a roll — the serial number showed that — and it was just about seven-thirty when the box-office girl put a new roll in the machine, or whatever the drill is. So that settles it. The boy must have gone there straight from the Grapevine. If he didn't kill Morningside, presumably he didn't kill Miss Quimper either. He's in quite enough trouble without that, unfortunately. Silcutt can't overlook it this time.'

'No,' said Johnny. Sally remembered his earlier arguments. Either Teddy or one of a limited group of intelligent people: Michael Knox, Selina, Miss Quimper, Toby, and Silcutt. The murderer was certainly the joker. It wasn't Teddy. It almost certainly wasn't Michael Knox. It wasn't Miss Quimper. It wasn't Selina, unless Johnny's whole theory of the case was wrong, and his theory was extremely convincing. But not Toby, she thought. Not Toby.

'In the second place,' Camberley was saying, 'the *Echo* switchboard told me that Miss Marvell was trying to find me, and Miss Marvell told me that you were trying to find me. What can I do for you, if it's not too late?'

Sally saw Johnny grow a little taut. 'It's very kind of you, sir,' he said. 'I wanted to ask you to go over the earlier part of Wednesday evening for me.'

Camberley blinked. Then he said sharply, 'Lorn? Are you serious?'

'I'm sufficiently serious to want his movements, sir.'

'But he was with Morningside and me all through the crucial period.'

'The canteen period. I'm not quite sure now that that is the crucial period.'

The Brigadier looked at him very hard. 'All right,' he said. 'You know what you're doing, I'm afraid. I'll start at six o'clock, shall I?'

'Please, sir.'

'At about six o'clock Lorn and I left Echo House. Mrs Heldar and Silcutt came down in the lift with us — I'd been with Silcutt in his office for the last half-hour or so. We parted from them outside the Fleet Street entrance and went along to the Old Fleet. Our actual destination, incidentally, wasn't prearranged, and it was my suggestion. I had asked Lorn half an hour before to join me in a drink somewhere nearby, and to meet me

in the entrance hall at six. In fact we met outside Silcutt's office, but that was mere chance. I had also mentioned to Lorn that I was going on to the House later,
and I think I made it clear to him then — that is, at half
past five or thereabouts — that before I went, I was
going to eat with Morningside in the canteen. I don't
think I told him then at what time we were eating. I'm
giving you these details in case they're of some use.

'In the Old Fleet, Lorn told me that you and he were
seeing Morningside in Peex at eight, and, as he was
going back to Echo House, I suggested he should eat
with Morningside and me in the canteen at a quarter to
seven. He agreed.

'In due course we returned to Echo House and went
straight down to the canteen. We reached it, as I think
Lorn told you, about a quarter to seven. Morningside
was already there. We ate, and Lorn told Morningside
about the conference at eight. His manner, incidentally,
seemed perfectly normal. He was rather tired — I think
he generally is after a long day — but that was all.
Morningside left us about a quarter past seven, and we
sat over our coffee for perhaps five minutes longer. I
told Lorn then that I should be tremendously interested
to attend your conference, but that I didn't want to
force myself upon you, and I asked him if he would ring
you up and find out what you felt about it. When we
left the canteen, he went off to do that, but I'm afraid I
don't know where he telephoned from. Perhaps
you do?'

'No,' said Johnny.

'Pity. We did touch briefly on that question. We
agreed that Lorn had better not use the telephone in his
own office, because of the glass hatch between his office and Morningside's, which as you know is not
soundproof. We also agreed that he shouldn't use any
Echo telephone, because we didn't particularly want the

conversation overheard by the *Echo* switchboard. He said he'd find a telephone somewhere and went off. He may have talked to you from one of the call boxes in the entrance hall, but he was a little doubtful about those; as he said, the *Echo*'s reporters are often hanging about there, and he might conceivably be overheard. I think it's more likely he went out and rang up from a call box in some pub.

'Well, in the meantime I was looking for Carfrae of the *Daily Echo*. I ran him to earth after a bit in someone else's office, had a chat with him, and got back to the entrance hall, where I'd agreed to meet Lorn, just before eight o'clock. About three minutes to, I think. He was there when I arrived. But you want to talk to Brown — the night-porter there. He may be able to give Lorn an alibi, and he's fairly discreet.'

'Yes. I must see him. Thank you very much, sir.'

'If you'd like to go tonight, I'll ring him up and tell him he can safely answer anything you ask him.'

'That's very good of you. I think perhaps I will go tonight.'

Sally was grateful to Camberley too. It would be better to get it over. Brown's evidence might tell against Toby, but if Johnny didn't get it tonight, he wouldn't sleep.

Camberley talked to Brown, who was obviously a friend of his. 'That's all right,' he said when he had rung off. 'He's expecting you. If you want to go now, we'll find a taxi and I'll drop you. What about you, Mrs Heldar? Are you going with your husband?'

'Yes,' said Sally quickly.

Before they reached Fleet Street, Camberley said, 'I don't want to ask awkward questions, but is Michael still in this?'

'No,' said Johnny. 'I've gone into him very carefully, and I don't see how he can possibly have done it.'

Camberley gave a little sigh. 'Thank God for that, anyway.'

'You know what was behind it all, I gather.'

'You mean I know what would have been his motive? Yes. He told me that story himself, some time ago. But he never mentioned Morningside's name; I only heard it much later in that connection. If he had mentioned it, I wouldn't have recommended him for this job. I don't mean that I should have expected him to do murder, but neither should I have expected him to deal wisely or discreetly with what was undoubtedly a very difficult situation. That poor wretched boy—'

'What happened to the girl?' asked Sally. She had wanted to know that ever since Silcutt had told them the story.

'He wanted to marry her, but she wouldn't have him. She felt, I gather, that their whole relationship had been vitiated and cheapened by Morningside's talebearing, and she was afraid that Dowd only wanted to make an honest woman of her. I don't know where she is now, but I hope he'll find her again someday. Well, here we are. I shall see you at the inquest tomorrow, I expect. Goodnight.'

The entrance hall was fortunately unoccupied, except by Brown. He welcomed them almost warmly and made them sit down on the red quilted seat. He was a little, bright, bird-like Cockney, Ortheris to Laxton's Learoyd.

'The Brigadier says I'm ter answer yer questions, sir, and not say nothink ter nobody. Right you are, sir. I'm ready.'

'Good,' said Johnny. 'Can you remember if Mr Lorn of the Archives telephoned from one of these call boxes round about half past seven on Wednesday evening — the evening Mr Morningside was killed?'

Brown, standing almost at attention in front of

Johnny, considered at some length. He wrinkled his forehead and screwed up his eyes in an intense effort to remember. At last he said, 'No. No, sir, I'm very sorry; I couldn't say. There's so many people uses them boxes.' He stopped suddenly. 'Of course. I wasn't 'ere abaht 'alf past seven that evenin'. I told the Brigadier that, and the perlice, when they was wantin' ter know wot time Miss Marvell left the buildin' after she came back. You 'eard abaht that, sir?'

'Yes. How long were you out of the hall, Brown?'

'Maybe ten minutes, sir. Say from abaht five minutes before the 'alf-hour till abaht five minutes after.'

'I see. Had you seen Mr Lorn just before that? Any time after a quarter past seven, say?'

'I don't think so, sir. Can't swear ter it, but I don't remember seein' 'im then.'

'And when did you next see him?'

Brown frowned again. 'The perlice arst me that, sir. 'E came inter the 'all just abaht five ter eight, as near as I can remember. And the Brigadier came and sat down beside 'im a couple o' minutes later. And then you and Mrs 'Eldar came in.'

'Thank you very much, Brown. That's all, I think. I'm much obliged to you.'

'Not at all, sir. Call you a cab, sir?'

'Please,' said Johnny.

* * *

HE SCARCELY SPOKE in the taxi. It was like their homecoming after Morningside's death. When they were back in the drawing room Sally knelt down on the hearthrug and woke up the drowsy fire with the bellows. Then she turned to Johnny, who was standing staring down at the rising flames.

'Sit down and talk, darling,' she said.

Johnny shivered a little and smiled faintly. 'Sorry,' he said, and sat down on the sofa. 'I was thinking about Peter.'

Sally knew he meant Peter Lorn. She picked up his tumbler, got him a neat whisky, and put it into his hand. He thanked her and drank.

'That's better,' he said. 'You're right. We've got to work it out. He could have done it, Sally. Wait a minute; we want the timetable.'

He pulled out his wallet, took out the table they had made, and unfolded it. Then he began to talk in an almost expressionless voice.

'When he left the canteen, about seven-twenty, he went straight up to Peex by the back lift, which has no operator. He entered Peex by the back way at seven-twenty-five — one minute after Selina had left it by the front way. Now, Camberley agreed that he'd asked Morningside for a *Reflector* cutting, but he couldn't remember if he'd asked him in the afternoon or while they were in the canteen. It was Toby who said he didn't remember his asking for it in the canteen. In fact he did remember, and he used it as a pretext to get Morningside out of Peex. He told Morningside that Camberley was in a hurry for it — just as Morningside told Miss Quimper a few minutes later. His leg would slow him down a bit' — Johnny's voice was suddenly harsh — 'but I think he could rig the trap in six minutes.

'Two or three minutes after the half-hour it was all over. And the moment it was over, Toby got through the hatch — difficult for him, but not impossible — and rang me up from his own office. A line was plugged in to his telephone from the Archives switchboard; he could get through without delay, and there was no one to listen in and remember where he had spoken from. It was unlikely that anyone would come into Peex;

Camberley was about the only possible person, and Toby had arranged to meet him downstairs at eight.

'As soon as Toby had talked to me, he went down and saw someone on the *Echo*. He told us himself a couple of days ago that just before he met us at eight, he was gossiping with someone on the *Echo*, when Knox's friend Wilson was sent off on a job.

'Very well, then. He had his alibi for the canteen period. But he had provided for the post-canteen period too. If he could only persuade everyone that he had telephoned to me from outside Echo House — and Camberley's evidence would support his statement — he would be perfectly safe. He had established a quite sound reason for not telephoning from the entrance hall, which might have given him just enough time to rig the trap. But it would be quite obvious that he couldn't have gone up to Peex, rigged the trap and got through the hatch, come down again, gone out into Fleet Street and found a telephone, and got through to me, between seven-twenty and about seven-thirty-three. He didn't know, of course, that Brown hadn't been in the entrance hall round about half past seven; that was a piece of luck for him. He would expect Brown to say that he hadn't noticed Mr Lorn going out or coming in about that time. But there's a good deal of coming and going, and Brown's evidence wouldn't seem very conclusive. No one, again, would have seen Toby telephoning from the pub of his choice, but pubs are busy places, and that wouldn't seem very conclusive either.

'He talked to me until, say, seven-thirty-seven or seven-thirty-eight. His friend on the *Echo* gives him an alibi from, say, just after seven-forty till after seven-fifty, and Brown says he was in the entrance hall at seven-fifty-five. So he couldn't possibly have done it.

'And please note this. His plan didn't depend on the

opportunities Camberley gave him. If Camberley hadn't asked him to come and have a drink, he'd have gone and had one himself. It was desirable to have an alibi for the pre-canteen period, because there would probably be no evidence that Morningside had been in his office between six o'clock and a quarter to seven, and we might ask ourselves if the trap hadn't been rigged then. At that time of the evening Toby would have been quite likely to find an acquaintance in any Fleet Street pub, and if he didn't, he could make one who would remember him. Again, if Camberley hadn't invited him to the canteen — and hadn't invited Morningside either — he would have invited Morningside himself. He'd chosen a Wednesday evening, when Morningside nearly always ate in the canteen in any case and went back to his office afterwards. Morningside wouldn't be there to give him his canteen-period alibi, but it would be astonishing if no one else could. Again, if Camberley hadn't mentioned the cutting, he could easily have found a pretext of his own to get Morningside out of Peex. After all, he was Morningside's departmental chief. Finally, if Camberley hadn't asked him to ring me up, he could have found some other reason for doing it, or he could have rung up someone else. But I was the most convenient person, because I was going to be questioned by the police anyway.'

'Stop a minute,' said Sally. 'Would he have arranged a conference with you for eight o'clock if he'd been planning to kill Morningside?'

Johnny's face lightened a little, and then darkened again.

'I think he might,' he said. 'If Morningside's body hadn't been found till the next morning, the evidence as to time of death would probably have been very indefinite indeed. I should think Toby would have had to carry his alibi on to midnight or after, if he was to be quite safe. He may have thought it easier and safer to limit the thing by having the body found at eight, and his movements apparently cut and dried. As it was, he deliberately suggested that Morningside had died about twenty past seven and killed him about twelve minutes after that. But the discrepancy was very slight, and the medical evidence more than justified it; the doctors got nowhere near as close as that.' Johnny thought for a moment, and then found his place in the argument.

'The great advantage of Camberley's intervention was that it shifted the initiative. Camberley organised the proceedings, not Toby, and Camberley's reputation is so great that his word would be worth almost as much as the word of a High Court judge.'

Sally nodded. 'Yes. But, Johnny, tell me this: if Toby wanted everyone to think he'd telephoned to you from a pub, why on earth didn't he tell you so at the time?'

Johnny thought for a moment, and then turned a little white.

'Because a pub means a penny-in-the-slot telephone,' he said quietly, 'and I hadn't heard the pennies drop.'

'Are you sure, darling?'

'I'm quite sure. I didn't hear any pennies drop. He was using an ordinary telephone. He couldn't risk telling me a lie about it at the time. He could only hope that by the time it came up I'd have forgotten there had been no pennies.'

Sally heard herself saying without her own volition, 'It can't be Toby. It can't be.'

'Who else could have done it, Sally? It fits in far too well. And he's very much in love with Selina. He may have realised that Morningside wanted to mend his engagement to her, and he may have had a sense of inferiority because of his leg. His mind may have got twisted—'

'Do you think he would really have killed Miss Quimper?'

'Well, he's got no alibi, and I think he's quite strong enough.'

'You didn't ask Brown if he saw him go out on Friday evening. He said himself that he left about six, didn't he?'

'Yes. I didn't ask Brown — I didn't think of it at the time — but he could have come back, you know. He could have slipped in by Laxton's door while Laxton was out on patrol, or he could even have got in and out by the coalhole. That would be difficult for him, again, but he can do almost anything if he makes up his mind to it. When he was a little younger, he used to do damn silly things with his leg just to prove to himself that he could.'

'Stop,' said Sally. 'Stop, darling. Miss Quimper's murder wasn't premeditated. The murderer just happened to overhear her talking to me. He didn't lay his plans in advance.'

Johnny looked at her, and the first real gleam of hope appeared in his eyes.

'I'm sorry,' he said. 'I was being stupid. If he did leave Echo House about six, I think he's in the clear.' Johnny added almost violently, 'I can't wait for this. Be damned to the *Echo* switchboard.'

He reached for the Telephone Directory, found the *Echo*'s number, and dialled it. When he was answered he asked for the entrance hall.

After a moment Brown's voice said, 'Night-porter front 'all.'

'Brown,' said Johnny, 'we had a talk this evening about the movements of a man we know. No names, please, but do you remember?'

'Yes, I remember, sir. Is there somethink else?'

'Yes, please. Can you remember when the man in question left on Friday evening?'

'Yessir. 'Baht six o'clock, it was, when the young gent left. And 'e didn't come back, neither.'

'You're quite sure?'

Brown was hurt by Johnny's sharpness. 'Quite sure, sir. It's me job ter remember when they goes aht and in. Besides, I've been all over them times with the perlice, and they're fresh in me memory, so ter speak. Father O'Flynn went off just before five-thirty, the marvellous girl rahnd abaht five-forty-five, the young gent abaht six, and the Big White Chief abaht ten ter seven.'

'All right,' said Johnny. 'I'm sorry. God bless you, Brown.'

'Thank you, sir,' said Brown, a little taken aback, 'and the same ter you, I'm sure.'

CHAPTER THIRTEEN

The inquest on Edith Quimper was held on the following morning. The doctors and Inspector Lindesay between them caused a sensation by making it clear — as far as the doctors were concerned, with a good deal of unpleasant detail — that the deceased had either fallen, thrown herself, or been thrown, from a sixth-floor window. Death might have taken place — again as far as the doctors were concerned — at any time between approximately four o'clock on Friday afternoon and ten o'clock on Friday night.

Evidence of identity was taken from Miss Quimper's married sister, and Laxton described his discovery of the body. Then Sally was called and questioned about her telephone conversation with the deceased. This, of course, provided a later *terminus a quo* than the doctors had been able to give. It also suggested, at any rate to the Press, which lost no time in passing the suggestion on to the public, that Miss Quimper had been murdered, and that because she had possessed some dangerous knowledge of Morningside's murderer. Again, and most unfortunately, it left no doubt in anyone's mind that Johnny was investigating the case.

The Coroner, however, pointed out to his jury that

the medical witnesses had made it clear that, so far as they were concerned, there was no conclusive evidence to show whether the deceased had met her death by misadventure, by her own act, or by some other person's. If the jury felt, as they well might, that no other evidence they had heard could be considered conclusive in this respect, they must bring in an open verdict. They did so without retiring.

Sally and Johnny got through the reporters with some difficulty and went home for lunch; Camberley had been there with Silcutt, but they were evidently lunching à deux. When the Heldars had eaten Johnny went on to the shop, saying he would probably be late that evening.

Two reporters visited St Cross Square in the course of the afternoon. Sally had asked Nanny to answer the front door, and Nanny appeared to deal with them successfully, probably by the simple expedient of treating them as rude little boys. When Johnny came home, after half past six, he said they had been to the Charing Cross Road too, and one of them had caught him in the shop.

'A tiresome afternoon,' he said. 'No, I don't think I'll have a drink, all the same. I've been pub-crawling again, and I've done myself quite well already.'

'More barmaids?' asked Sally resignedly.

'Several,' said Johnny with gusto. 'Well — in point of fact — two. Or, to be strictly accurate, one and a landlord's wife.'

'That's rather worse.'

'Yes, isn't it?' He grinned and paused to light a cigarette.

'I wanted to be quite sure about Toby,' he said, 'so I looked for an explanation of his telephone call. I tried the pubs nearest to Echo House, and I struck lucky with my second one — the Old Fleet. That was where I

185

got off with the landlord's wife. She's nice and cosy, with a vein of pantomime humour, and she knows Toby. He was there with Camberley on Wednesday evening from about six till nearly a quarter to seven. But he came back about half past seven, and she saw him waiting for the penny-in-the-slot telephone off the bar, with two or three people ahead of him. He looked very tired, and was dragging his leg, and she was so sorry for him that she took him into her own sitting room, where there's another telephone — not a penny-in-the-slot type. She left him alone with that, and when he came out, they had an argument about his paying for the call. He won and paid, and then went away. That was about twenty to eight. He can't have reached his friend on the *Echo* before a quarter to, and he can't possibly have stayed for a word with him and murdered Morningside as well. And that's that.

'Well, now. Knox didn't kill Morningside. Teddy — didn't kill Morningside. Miss Quimper didn't kill Morningside and then commit suicide. Toby, praise God, didn't do it, and I'm pretty sure Selina didn't.'

'So what?' asked Sally.

Johnny said slowly, 'Sherlock Holmes said that when you had eliminated the impossible, whatever remained, *however improbable*, must be the truth.'

'But no one remains,' said Sally. Then she stared at him. 'Johnny, that's impossible, surely. I kept on remembering him at the beginning, and you kept on snubbing me.'

'I know. I apologise. But it's not impossible. He hasn't got an alibi for either of the murders, and Brown told us last night that he'd left about ten to seven on Friday evening. The only thing that worries me is that he ought to have an alibi for the canteen period, and he says he just went home.'

'Wait a minute!' said Sally urgently. 'Wait a minute!'

She put her hands over her eyes and thought. The picture took gradual shape. A busy street corner, and under a lighted lamp a magnificent man getting into a taxi, and giving the driver an address in a small, precise voice.

She looked up and said, 'He didn't go straight home. He hurried on ahead of me, but when I reached the corner of St Barnabas' Lane he was getting into a taxi. I heard him tell the man to go to Merchant Hatters' Buildings in Holborn, on the corner of Silk Street.'

'Well done,' said Johnny. 'Damn it, we ought to have a Post Office Directory here. I think I'll go and have a look at the place now.'

'I'll come with you. It's Shepherd's Pie for supper. Nanny can help herself and turn down the oven.'

* * *

THEY TOOK a taxi to a point some way east of Kingsway, and then walked on to Silk Street. It was very near St Barnabas' Lane, and Sally suspected that Silcutt had taken a taxi only in order to get well away from her. The ground floor of Merchant Hatters' Buildings consisted of two shops: a very ordinary chemist's and an unoriginal stationer's. They probably both shut at six or before, and in any case, it seemed unlikely that Silcutt had come off his usual beat to visit either. But the big door between them stood open, and beside it was a row of nameplates. Johnny took them from the bottom up.

'Dentist. I hardly think so. I think he'd go to Harley Street, even if this man is open after six. Typing and duplicating — possibly. He may write, for all we know, and they may work late sometimes. Insurance brokers — possibly, again. Isaac Rothstein, Financier — unlikely. Dressmaker — no. Miss Désirée Molyneux, Teacher of Dancing. I wonder.'

They looked at each other, and Sally said, 'You remember what Selina told Toby — that he couldn't dance, but he was much more of a ladies' man than you'd think. Do you think he's learning to dance for Selina's sake?'

'Men have done more for less. Come on; we'll go and see.'

They went into a narrow, stone-paved hall lined with sage-green tiles. An iron lift-cage rose in the well of the stone staircase, but they walked up. On the first-floor landing there were two doors, both with panels of frosted glass. No light showed behind either. On the second floor the insurance brokers' office was in darkness, but Mr Rothstein's was dimly lit.

Already they had begun to hear strains of music coming from above. When they reached the top of the last flight, they saw an open door — open, perhaps, to let some air into the lighted room beyond. A woman's voice, agonisingly refined, was raised in a sort of ritual chant.

'...And — *forward* side close and — *forward* side close and — *one* two three and — *one* two three and — *turn* two three and — *back* two three — *back*, Mr Rivington, please; you'll have me into the wall — and — *back* two three and — *back* two three — very well, Mr Rivington; we'll *rest* two three.'

The Heldars had reached the door and looked in. They saw a smallish room, with a rather overwhelming contemporary wallpaper. At the far end was a little table with a gramophone on it and a chair on either side. The instructress — presumably Miss Molyneux herself — and her partner were just separating. The partner was a perspiring young man in a not very well-cut suit. He caught sight of the Heldars from behind the handkerchief with which he was mopping his brow, and his discomfort became acute. He was far too red in the face to blush, but he looked as if, given the slightest encouragement, he would run away, and Sally was sorry for him.

Miss Molyneux turned off the gramophone and came to the door. She was short and plump, and dressed in a black pleated skirt, a frilly white blouse, and a good deal of costume jewellery. Her carefully set hair was grey, and her face suggested a monkey which had put on weight. But she moved with a lovely fluent grace which in a younger and slimmer woman would have been breath taking, and even in her held the eye.

'I'm so sorry,' she said in her ridiculous voice. 'I'm full up till Christmas. I do wish I could help you, but I can't. Not till January, I mean. I'd be delighted to take you then, but you would need to put your names down now.'

'That's very kind of you,' said Johnny, 'but I'm afraid we were just looking for a friend. We must find him this evening, and we thought he'd be here, but he doesn't seem to be. His name's Silcutt.'

She shook her head, and her elaborate earrings swung furiously to and fro.

'What a pity!' she said. 'This isn't his evening, you know; he comes on Wednesday. Wednesday from a quarter past six till a quarter past seven.'

'Oh, how silly of us!' said Sally. 'I believe he did say Wednesday. He was with us on Thursday evening, and he said he'd been here the evening before.'

'Come to think of it, I believe he did,' said Johnny. 'Or did he say something about having cancelled it or changed it, or cut it short, or something?'

'Oh, no,' said Miss Molyneux. 'He came last Wednesday — it was his second lesson — and he came at the right time and stayed till a quarter past seven. He's very punctual, and very persevering; I think there must be a young lady somewhere.'

'That would be telling,' said Sally, making an effort to fall in with this archness, and Miss Molyneux gave a genteel little giggle.

'I'm so sorry,' said Johnny. 'We've disturbed you for nothing.'

'Not at all; we're just resting. I do hope you find Mr Silcutt.'

'We will. Later in the evening, I expect. Thank you so much.'

They walked a little way westward, and then picked up another taxi. When they were moving Sally said, 'I can't help thinking this is suspicious. What's Lionel Silcutt doing in a place like that? If he really wanted to learn dancing, he'd go to the West End.'

'Not necessarily,' said Johnny. 'If he's innocent, he's keeping this a close secret because it doesn't accord with his dignity, and it's quite natural that he should have hesitated to ask any of his friends to recommend a place. In that case he probably picked Wednesday because it's his housekeeper's evening out. If, on the other hand, he's guilty, this was a deliberately established alibi for the canteen period — he only started these lessons a week before Morningside was killed — and it had to be somewhere quite near Echo House. He couldn't have danced in the West End till a quarter past seven and got back in time to rig the trap at twenty-five past.'

'Why hasn't he produced his alibi?'

'He may possibly have given it to the police. But I think he'd have told me too, even if he hadn't wanted to admit it to Toby. If he's guilty, I fancy he's doing a little as we thought Knox was — being reticent about his movements so that his alibi will be more effective when it does come out. Only the innocent, as a rule, dare to lie when the lie is not to their advantage.'

Sally considered. 'He'd know in advance that Morningside would almost certainly be in the canteen while he was dancing, and I dare say Camberley told him before six that Morningside was eating with him. He probably didn't know that Camberley wanted a cutting, but Morningside was probably looking for it when he arrived in Peex. In any case he could have invented a reason for getting Morningside out of the way. But, Johnny, *why*? What motive could he conceivably have had?'

'I'll tell you what I think about that later,' said Johnny with a curious diffidence.

Just before supper, when she walked into the drawing room, he was on the telephone. She heard him say obscurely, 'Comic policemen? How very interesting. Well, thank you very much...Yes. I think it may be important.'

* * *

BUT IT WAS ONLY after supper that he explained.

'Yesterday afternoon,' he said, 'when we were in Peex, Teddy came up from the dark-room with some prints. They were obviously prints from some of the old negs Morningside had been examining, and one of them at least had apparently been destined to his "Myself when Young" series, which Toby mentioned when he first told us about this business. Well, do you remember what Teddy said yesterday? "Might 'ave murdered 'im meself if I thought 'e was all set to publish one like that of me."'

'Darling,' said Sally, 'I know Lionel Silcutt's a pompous little Civil Servant with an exaggerated idea of his own importance and a very tender dignity. But surely — surely he wouldn't commit murder in order not to appear in public in a sailor-suit.'

'Oh, no. No man in or near his senses would do that. But supposing Silcutt when young had been or done something which he couldn't afford to have known today.'

Sally frowned. 'It still doesn't make sense,' she said. 'If it hadn't been known before, how could a photograph give it away?'

'Well,' said Johnny almost apologetically, 'it would mean that he'd been or done it under another name, you know. But Morningside had a remarkable gift for spotting people in old photographs. Supposing he happened on a picture of, shall we say, a notorious forger who had never been arrested, and recognised it as his chief. You know what he was. He wouldn't have hesitated to expose him, if the thing was sufficiently serious.'

Sally shook her head. 'I can't believe it. Silcutt's so intensely respectable.'

'I know,' said Johnny. 'I know. It's far-fetched; it's fantastic if you like. But it's the only motive I can think of. And none of the others murdered Morningside, and in view of the persecution it can hardly have been anyone from outside the Archives.'

'But he wouldn't have to do murder. He'd only have to get hold of the neg and destroy it. And the pic if there was one.'

'I don't think there were any pix corresponding to these old negs, except those that Morningside ordered. I've no doubt the murderer tried to destroy the neg. It was probably he who messed up the old negs looking for it. Morningside didn't deny that he had touched them, but from what Miss Quimper said, he was so tired and upset when she tackled him that he may not have been sure what negs he'd touched and what he hadn't.'

Sally was still unconvinced. 'But, Johnny, there's no evidence for all this, is there?'

'Well — there's an indication. Pretty slight, I admit.

When Selina told us how she waited for Morningside in his office while he was in the canteen, she said she'd looked at one or two of the old negs he was working on. I remembered, when she said it, that when we found the body there were no glass negs in the office except those which had been spilt from the box, and I noted the point as a possible indication that she might be lying — though on balance I was fairly certain her story was true. Before supper this evening I rang her up and asked her if she could be more specific about the negs she'd looked at. She said that on second thoughts there had been only one, and that it had been in the tray where Morningside put old negs he was inclined to keep. It had been a group of people — men or boys — dressed as comic policemen. Yes, you can laugh if you like. But when we found Morningside dead that neg was gone — I looked at his desk and I know. I believe the murderer removed it. Anyway, Sally, I'm going to ring up Toby and ask him if there's any chance of finding out the subject matter of that lot of negs. If I'm right, you see, we're working against time to some extent. Silcutt's lesson is tomorrow evening, and Désirée is almost bound to tell him we were asking for him. And once he gets our descriptions from her, he'll know it was us — that's why I didn't bother to put on a more elaborate act. But it won't be fatal, of course; he established his alibi in order to use it if necessary.'

He dialled Toby's number. He didn't tell Toby whom he suspected but explained his theory of the motive without attaching it to any particular person. Then he asked his question.

'Well, not exactly,' said Toby. 'Those particular negs weren't labelled, and there's no catalogue — it was lost in the Blitz. So, incidentally, if Morningside found a picture of Charlie, the Cat-Burglar No One Can Catch, he'd have to recognise it as such for himself — perhaps from the background or some other part of the context — as well as recognising it as his esteemed colleague Mr Lorn. But there is one chance: the bags. All these old negs were packed in paper bags to preserve them, and each bag has a label stuck on it with the number of the neg — the number given it by its original owners, that is. And now and then there's a note as well as the number. You might just get a clue to the Policemen's Chorus there. The bags were removed in Negs, but Miss Quimper always kept them at least until Morningside had been through the stuff, just in case they were wanted, and I don't suppose she threw out the last lot. She very seldom threw anything out. And her assistants haven't done much on their own initiative since she died.'

'Could you find those bags for me tonight, Toby?'

'I could certainly try,' said Toby, 'if it's urgent.'

'It may be,' said Johnny.

* * *

THEY FOUND Toby talking to Laxton twenty minutes later. Laxton wished them good evening as they came in. His eyes were placid now, but he was interested by this late visit.

In Negs, with its fluorescent lighting, it might have been any hour. Toby looked over Miss Quimper's desk and explored its drawers. Then he scuffed over to a table against the wall; his leg was dragging even more than it generally did at night.

'Here we are,' he said, and scuffed back with a wire tray. In it were three small bundles of old semi-transparent bags, each of them secured by a rubber band. Under each band was a slip of paper on which was written:

Negs to Mr Morningside 26/11/58. EQ.

The men pulled up chairs, and they all sat down round Miss Quimper's desk. They took a bundle each and began to look through the bags.

The labels were a little dusty, and the numbers were written in faded ink. And now and then, as Toby had said, there was a note. By Johnny's advice, they put all the bags with notes aside. But there was nothing that seemed to mean very much. The most usual form was: 'Take print for *Daily Echo*' — or for Smith's or Brown's or whoever the client happened to be — followed by someone's initials and a long-ago date.

But after ten minutes Sally found something and looked up suddenly. She said nothing for a moment, but Johnny and Toby looked up too, as if her excitement had communicated itself to them. She showed them the note.

Take copy neg for CID.
  NB Moustache of figure in foreground to be touched out.
  EQ.
  16/2/28.

'My God!' said Johnny. He sounded not so much excited as astonished, and Toby looked at him interrogatively.

'Didn't you expect something like this?'

'I didn't really expect anything. It seemed too much to hope for, even if I was right. Of course this may not have anything to do with the Policemen's Chorus — though comic policemen usually wear moustaches — but even so—'

'Even so, I imagine the CID want photographs for one reason and one reason only,' said Toby. He paused. 'This is Miss Quimper's note. The murderer probably realised she might have had something to do with the neg in her Evans's days. He may have killed her in case she remembered it — and in case she'd seen it again recently — as well as because he was worried by her conversation with Sally.'

Johnny nodded. 'But he didn't realise that the note would be here,' he said. 'Well, I'm going to take it to Scotland Yard.'

Toby said nothing more for the moment. He was frowning, and Sally guessed that he was making calculations. He himself hadn't been born in nineteen-twenty-eight. Nor had Selina; nor had Teddy. Michael Knox had been a child or a schoolboy. Sally saw the look of incredulous enlightenment come into Toby's face.

CHAPTER FOURTEEN

The next day was a long and anxious one, punctuated by occasional visits from the Press. The police could hardly be expected to sort out Silcutt's past in a matter of twenty-four hours, but the Heldars hoped to hear something before long about the note they had found. When the front-door bell rang while they were washing up after supper, Sally had an idea it might be Lindesay. But it was Toby, wanting news badly and feeling that their house was the most likely place for it.

They sat in the drawing room and did *The Times* crossword to take their minds off the case. They had nearly finished it when the bell rang again. But again it wasn't Lindesay. It was Camberley, and he came into the room as if he were glad to be back.

Johnny must have told him on the way upstairs that he could talk freely in Toby's presence, for he didn't hesitate. But it was clear that he didn't like what he had to say. He looked worried and tired, and for the first time Sally realised that the strain of this business was telling on him.

'My friend Superintendent Wigram,' he said, 'sent for me today to ask me what I knew about Silcutt. I didn't know very much. I met him for the first time a little under a year ago, when he was appointed to the Archives. We went into him then, of course, and everything we learnt was satisfactory. But really my knowledge doesn't go far enough back to touch the main issue. The police are digging hard. They've already unearthed a rather interesting story — though so far it seems to have no connection with Silcutt — which I think I may tell you in confidence. It's in their records under the date of the note you found, and there are men at Scotland Yard who remember the case — Wigram himself is one of them. They remember it because, through no fault of their own, it was one of their failures.

'Early in nineteen-twenty-eight a young man called William Smith was living in South London. He was twenty years old, and he worked as a clerk in a City office. He had been orphaned as a child, and adopted by a maiden aunt, with whom he still lived. He had been educated at a local grammar school, where he had done very well, and had shown, in particular, a considerable talent for amateur theatricals. He had probably concealed this talent from his aunt, for she was a Nonconformist of the narrowest type and would never have consented to his appearance on any stage. One of his masters said that he had wanted very much to become a professional actor, and it seems possible that he quarrelled with his aunt over that. In any case, the evidence of the neighbours made it clear that they had been on bad terms. Miss Smith was rigid in her views, a powerful personality, and extremely possessive. The boy had no life and no friends of his own, outside his office.

'On the morning of the fifth of February, he opened the back door to the milkman and told him that his aunt had gone off the night before to Brighton, where her widowed sister had been taken ill, and would probably not be back for at least a week. He himself was going to share the digs of a friend at the office, and the milk should be stopped until further notice. Later in the morning the baker's roundsman found a notice on the gate saying: "No more bread till further notice, please." A local constable saw it too, so the police didn't worry about the house being shut.

'On the same morning someone rang up young Smith's office, professed to be his aunt, and said he was laid up with food poisoning and would be off work for at least a week. The girl who took the call was quite sure, at the time, that the caller was a woman, but you'll remember that Smith was a clever amateur actor.

'So no one worried for about ten days. And then the balloon went up. The local postman had heard the Brighton story from Miss Smith's neighbours, who had heard it from the milkman. When he woke up to the fact that since Miss Smith's departure, he had delivered two letters with the Brighton postmark, and addressed in a hand he'd been seeing for years, he mentioned it to the police. Enquiries in Brighton proved that she wasn't there and that her sister was in excellent health. The police broke into her house and found her in the cupboard under the stairs. She had been struck repeatedly on the head, probably with a poker.

'It was too late to tell to within a day or two when she had died, but there could be no reasonable doubt that her nephew had killed her. Apart from the other evidence, there were no signs of breaking and entering — although there was no money in the house — and no signs of a struggle. Various people who travelled on his usual train to the City had seen him on the fifth with a small suitcase, and he had told one or two of them the Brighton story, but after that, except for the telephone call, he had vanished into thin air. And no one has ever heard anything more of him.'

Camberley paused. 'I forgot to mention the photograph,' he said. 'It was a group taken by an Evans's photographer of some boys at Smith's school in *The Pirates of Penzance*. Smith appeared as the Sergeant of Police, wearing a false moustache. He had a good baritone, it seems. The photograph was over three years old — he was seventeen at the time — but the police couldn't do any better. If there had been any photographs of him in his aunt's house, he had had the forethought to remove them. What was more, he had actually removed his fingerprints from every single object in the house. It must have taken him hours, but it secured his future — or so he must have hoped. His office happened to be an old-fashioned sort of place where three or four clerks worked at the same desk, and the police never got any really good prints there either.'

Toby said slowly, 'So there was nothing but that one photograph. The copy in the CID files was unlikely to be dangerous, because no one at Scotland Yard knows him — except Lindesay — and as far as we know no one at Scotland Yard has Morningside's memory. But our copy was dangerous. Morningside was quite capable of seeing a man of fifty, whom he knew well, in the photograph of a boy of seventeen. I don't mean he could do it in any given case; some people change beyond recognition. But most people don't, and Smith was evidently photographed when he was made up as a grown man. Anyway, there was something almost uncanny about Morningside's gift.'

There was a long silence. Then Toby spoke again.

'Silcutt told me once that he lost his parents when he was very young and had no near relations.'

Camberley nodded. 'According to his record, he never went to a public school — or any school. He was delicate as a boy, and he had a tutor. He went up to Magdalen, but rather late.'

There was another silence. Sally was thinking how magnificent Silcutt must have looked as the Sergeant of Police.

* * *

ON THE FOLLOWING morning Johnny remembered a customer of Heldar Brothers who had probably been up at Magdalen with Silcutt and was reliable and discreet. He rang up at half past ten to tell Sally he had got in touch with Vaughan and been asked to lunch.

Sally went to tea with Aunt Margaret Heldar in Kensington, largely in order to avoid the Press, and didn't hurry home, because Johnny had said he was behindhand with his work at the shop and would probably be late. She let herself into the house a little after six, and met Nanny coming out of the kitchen with the children's supper trays.

'Good evening, madam,' said Nanny. 'Miss Marvell and Mr Toby are in the drawing room, and I've lit the fire. They've only been here about ten minutes.'

'Oh, thank you, Nanny,' said Sally, and went quickly upstairs. She crossed the first-floor landing to the drawing room door, and then stopped abruptly. Nanny hadn't quite closed it, and Selina's voice was clear even when it trembled.

'...And I was so *beastly* to you on Friday. I said such nasty cheap things — just to hurt you. I went into the Ladies' afterwards and cried my eyes out. I love you so much, Toby, and I'm not nearly nice enough for you.'

'My darling—' said Toby in an unrecognisable voice, and Sally turned swiftly away and followed Nanny upstairs.

When she went down again, she gave them fair warning by calling up to Nanny from the first floor and found them sitting decorously one at either end of the sofa and looking slightly dazed. It appeared that Toby was still hoping for news and had brought Selina with him. Sally said Johnny might come home with some information, and dispensed sherry.

But when Johnny came in, he looked a little worried.

'Vaughan knew Silcutt quite well,' he said. 'He never met him before Oxford. But he remembers an occasion on which a friend of Silcutt's father came up — a respectable solicitor who had known the family for years.'

'Does that mean we're wrong?' asked Sally.

'I don't know. I rang up Scotland Yard to pass it on to Lindesay, for what it's worth, but he was out for the afternoon, so I said I'd ring up again tomorrow.'

Toby and Selina didn't appear to take much of this in. Sally asked them, as a gesture, to stay to supper, and made it easy for them to refuse.

After supper Camberley came to St Cross Square with Superintendent Wigram. He had been told about Johnny's telephone call and had brought Wigram round to hear whatever news there was. When Johnny apologised for bringing them out for a very small matter, he smiled and said, 'Well, I really wanted you two to meet. I'd like to explode the theory that the professional and the amateur never really work together, no matter what the detective stories say.'

After that the evening went quite well. Camberley was obviously on terms of real friendship with this large elderly man with the friendly face. Wigram belonged to the world into which the Brigadier had been born, and Sally was pleased to see that he hadn't left it too far behind him.

Johnny repeated Vaughan's information, going into some detail, and Wigram nodded.

'I'm afraid,' he said, 'that's all of a piece with what we've learnt elsewhere. It's not difficult to put together the past of a man of his kind, and we've found one or two people who knew him as a child. It looks as if we're wrong. And yet I was certain you'd got the right motive, and there's no one else of the right age.'

Sally said suddenly, 'Haven't we been thinking all this time of Smith as creating Silcutt and inventing his past? Supposing there was a real Silcutt — a quiet, delicate boy whom not many people knew, and Smith took his identity from him? There would have had to be a physical resemblance, of course.'

'It might have been done,' said Johnny doubtfully. 'And we know Smith was a good actor. But there's a difference between playing the Sergeant of Police in *The Pirates* for an evening or two and playing a real Lionel Silcutt for life.'

'Was it the Sergeant in *The Pirates*?' asked Wigram. 'I don't think I ever heard that.' He broke unexpectedly and quite unselfconsciously into appropriate song, revealing a nice tenor.

'When the enterprising burglar's not a-burgling—'

Johnny and Camberley joined in an octave lower, *'Not a-burgling—'*

'When the cut-throat isn't occupied in crime—'

''Pied in crime—' sang Camberley.

'He loves to hear the little brook a-gurgling—'

'Brook a-gurgling—'

'And listen to the merry village chime—'

'Village chime—' growled Camberley.

Johnny rose suddenly to his feet. He spoke harshly, interrupting the Superintendent, who had gone on to the coster jumping on his mother.

'How did *you* know it was the Sergeant in *The Pirates*, Camberley?'

The next few minutes were nightmarish. In a sudden silence Sally saw Camberley's ruddy face distorted. After what seemed a long time his mouth opened under his moustache and he said in a voice whose mild surprise was so studied that no one could have believed in it, 'I must have heard it at Scotland Yard.'

'No, you didn't,' said Wigram. 'I never knew it, or if I did, I'd forgotten it. The photograph doesn't give a clue; it's just the usual stage uniforms. Might be any comic policemen. If they told us at the school what the show was, I didn't remember; it wasn't important. I don't think anyone else at Scotland Yard remembered it either, and anyway you didn't see anyone but me when you were there yesterday.'

His flat tones were curiously convincing and curiously menacing. 'Come to think of it,' he added, 'the photo's not unlike you.'

There was another silence, while the two men continued to stare at Camberley. Sally stared too, but after a moment she turned her head and looked at Johnny. What she saw frightened her. His eyes were merciless, and his mouth was set in an immovable determination. She looked at Camberley again, and saw him as another man. His pleasant, familiar features seemed to have dislimned, his mouth was open, and fear looked out of his eyes.

When he rose, the movement was so sudden that they were all taken by surprise. Wigram was a heavy man, and out of training, and it took him a moment to get out of his chair. Johnny moved instinctively between Camberley and Sally. If he had gone straight for the man he would probably have been in time, but the side-step held him up for a second. Camberley, who was nearest the door, reached it two paces ahead of him, whipped out, and held it just long enough to turn the key on the outside. They heard him crashing down the stairs.

'His car's outside,' said Wigram.

Johnny put his mouth to the keyhole and roared, 'Nanny!' He added more quietly, 'We needn't get in a flap; we shan't catch him anyway. We'd better try for his number.'

Sally had run to the nearest window and drawn back a curtain. She saw the big figure cross the pavement and leap into the long, low car which stood at the kerb. The engine started, and the car shot forward. The light from the nearest streetlamp fell on the rear number plate, and Johnny, beside her, read the number aloud and went to write it down on the telephone pad.

The door opened. 'Whatever's happening, madam?' asked Nanny reprovingly. 'You were locked in, and the key's gone. I had to take the one from your bedroom door. I heard Mr Heldar call out and someone running downstairs. If you're playing noisy games, I'm afraid you'll waken the children.' She stopped as a drowsy wail drifted down from above. 'There now, that's Peter. Excuse me, madam.'

Wigram's face, which was greyish, broke into a faint smile. Then he said, 'I'll use your phone, if I may.'

Johnny put an arm round Sally and they waited while the Superintendent issued sharp orders — all the sharper, she thought, because of the savage personal blow which had just been dealt him.

When he had finished Johnny said quietly, 'I apologise to both of you. I had no right to take things into my own hands like that, and one doesn't as a rule tackle a murderer in one's wife's drawing room. But you see, there was no evidence against him, and there never would have been. The only chance was to stampede him.'

'Yes,' said Wigram heavily. 'Well, we'll talk about that when we've caught him. Tell me, Mr Heldar, did you work it all out while we were singing?'

'Oh, no. I'd realised that he could have murdered

Morningside and Miss Quimper, and that he could be Smith. But I couldn't believe it till he gave himself away. I spent the time while you were singing trying to decide what to do.'

Wigram nodded. Then he said he must get back to Scotland Yard, and Johnny took him downstairs and came back to Sally.

'The policeman's lot is not a happy one,' he said.

'Nor is the amateur investigator's, my darling. They will catch him, I suppose?'

'Unless he smashes himself up, they're bound to. And then there'll be a trial, and he'll have a very good chance of getting off. But there'll be no future for him.'

CHAPTER FIFTEEN

The next morning Toby rang Sally up.

'I've been trying to get Johnny at the shop,' he said quickly, 'but they say he's with a customer. Sally, you've heard that Camberley was killed in a motor accident at Hammersmith last night? Ran himself into a brick wall?'

'Yes,' said Sally.

'There's a buzz going round Fleet Street that he did it deliberately, because he was involved in our affair. You know what I mean, damn it, and I'm not asking as a newspaperman. Is it true?'

'Yes,' said Sally. 'He was involved, and the police are fairly certain it was deliberate. Would you like to come to supper, Toby? And bring Selina?'

* * *

As it happened, Toby came without Selina. Her mother was in London, he said, and Sally guessed that Selina had some explaining to do. But it oughtn't to be very difficult. The son of a country rectory was something that Mrs Marvell would be able to understand, and after poor Morningside he would probably come to her as a great relief.

After supper they sat down round the fire, and Sally and Toby looked hard at Johnny.

'All right,' he said. 'Give me a moment to collect my thoughts.'

Then he began.

'Camberley,' he said, 'was of course Smith. He murdered his aunt and got away with it — it seems likely he managed to board some ship and leave the country, but we shall never know that. He doesn't come into the picture again until the outbreak of war in nineteen-thirty-nine, when he joined the army as James Camberley. I dare say it was safe enough; he was a man of over thirty, probably a good deal bigger and more mature than the City clerk of twenty, and probably, by that time, wearing a moustache. He was quite fearless and extremely ambitious, and no doubt he saw opportunities in joining up.

'Well, you know that story. Promotion, decorations, every possible success, until at the end of the war he was a national hero. Then he turned to other things. Journalism, authorship, politics — and again every success. He was even knighted. He was of course a brilliant actor, and he minimised his risks. He never pretended to be anything but what he was — a man who had risen from the ranks. He told us he'd been brought up in a flat over a grocer's shop, and that was part of the past he'd invented for himself — in fact his father was an innkeeper in a West Country town. So if he made the usual sort of social *gaffe*, no one worried. The general attitude was: "All honour to him for getting so far."

'He had very little to fear at first. Presumably he had had a copy of the *Pirates* group and had destroyed it after his aunt's death. Presumably he remembered that it had borne the name of Evans. But I gather a lot of

Evans's stuff was destroyed in the Blitz, and he probably hoped his photograph had gone too. Could he have
been certain it was among the stuff you took over,
Toby?'

'Virtually certain,' said Toby. 'Miss Quimper was
able to date the salvaged stuff very accurately by the
neg numbers.'

'I see. Well, he wasn't happy about Morningside's
memory, and he remembered that as the Sergeant of
Police he had been made up as a man and had worn a
moustache. He wore a moustache now.'

'His first idea, obviously, was to extract the neg before it got to Morningside and destroy it. He was already taking a keen interest in the Archives, and it was
easy to keep close to the staff and learn the procedure
they followed with the old negs. But looking for the
right one was a lengthy and difficult business. He had
to watch his chance and hurry through the stuff in
Negs when no one was there to see him or likely to interrupt him. It was probably he who messed up the old
negs last week — and no doubt on other occasions — as
we thought a little while ago that Silcutt had done. He
borrowed the cotton gloves so as not to leave fingerprints, but he couldn't help leaving traces of some sort,
because the bags were dusty. Unless he'd dusted the
whole lot—'

'No,' said Toby. 'Miss Quimper never let anyone but
herself touch them before they went up to Morningside, and her fads were pretty well known. But Camberley probably knew that any interference would be
attributed to Morningside. He knew a hell of a lot
about our staff troubles, because people naturally con-
fided in him.'

Johnny nodded, and went on. 'He'd always realised
that it might come to murder — he was entirely callous,
of course — and he instituted the persecution of Morn-

ingside in case it did. A series of increasingly unpleasant incidents which might culminate in a fatal
practical joke perpetrated by a joker who had become
insane. Pat's and Pam's rude rhymes and Teddy's prep
school stuff inspired him, and he prevented Silcutt
from sacking Teddy after the abduction of his car because he wanted the boy there as a suspect if Morningside had to die. He didn't know, of course, about the
Longwall business, which was going to give Teddy a
motive. He also recommended Michael Knox for an
Archives job, knowing that Knox had a record of violence (knocking down one's editor is not quite the same
thing as killing a man in cold blood, but it was better
than nothing), knowing he was precisely the type to get
on bad terms with Morningside, and knowing the
Dowd story.'

Sally interrupted. 'Camberley said that Michael
never told him it was Morningside who had been involved with Terence Dowd.'

'Camberley didn't want us to start wondering why
he'd recommended Knox — he who was such a judge
of men. I've no doubt Knox did tell him, but it would
have been his word against Camberley's. We were left
to assume that Silcutt had told Camberley. Of course
Camberley persuaded Silcutt to come out with the
Dowd story; Silcutt could be trusted not to admit that
he couldn't take his own decisions. And if, on the
strength of that and various little suggestions from
Camberley, we suspected the poor man, so much the
better.

'The persecution went quite well. It was of course
Camberley who acquired the key to Morningside's office. He was quite sufficiently intelligent and well-read
to produce the ruder rhymes, and he always delivered
them — and later on the letters — by hand, so that one
of the staff should appear to be responsible. He deliv-

ered a letter during the lunch-hour on the first day Sally watched Morningside's office.'

'Good Lord!' said Toby. 'I saw him go in myself. He said he wanted a picture.'

'So you told us. Well, at last he realised he wasn't going to be able to extract the neg. Morningside was getting through the stuff quicker than he could hope to do, and he knew it was time for his final joke. He was able to pick a Wednesday, when Morningside would almost certainly be working late, and luckily for him there was a box of negs in Morningside's office. He admitted just after we found the body that he'd known that. But he'd have found some other weapon if he'd been put to it.

'He asked you to have a drink with him, Toby, because he thought it safer to have an alibi for the pre-canteen period. But after that you became a serious complication. Obviously, you had to eat somewhere before your conference at eight. You might or might not eat in the canteen, but in either case you were quite likely to go up to Peex while he was rigging or springing the trap, and spoil everything. He decided that it would be better to have some idea of your movements than none, and that if he asked you to join him and Morningside in the canteen you would at least continue to help him with his alibi. The original idea was, of course, that in the normal course of establishing the victim's movements the police would establish the murderer's alibi.

'Someone who knew them both by sight would probably see them together. You would make that certain.

'After supper he asked you to telephone to me. He had deliberately not suggested your doing it from the Old Fleet earlier on, because he wanted it to occupy you now. He also made fairly certain that you would go out to do it, because that would take you longer. He arranged to meet you in the entrance hall at eight, and he hoped very hard that you were tired and wouldn't go upstairs first.'

A reasonable hope, thought Sally, in spite of the lifts. Toby's leg had been very tired indeed.

Toby was looking slightly embarrassed. 'Yes,' he said. 'He told me to take it easy. One rather did as he said.'

'That was one of his greatest assets. Incidentally, when I was silly enough to tell him that I knew the canteen period wasn't the crucial one, he saw at once that your alibi was now useless and that you might be made another red herring. He remembered that Brown had been out of the hall for a few minutes round about half past seven, and so probably wouldn't be able to say you'd gone out.'

'And if I hadn't gone out to telephone, I could have rigged the trap.'

'Quite so. His own story was that when you had left him, he looked for a man called Carfrae, on the *Daily Echo*, found him, apparently, with some difficulty, had a chat with him, and rejoined you in the entrance hall. I imagine it's perfectly possible to spend ten minutes or a quarter of an hour looking for someone in Echo House.

'In fact he went straight up to Peex by the back lift, and it was then that he asked Morningside for the *Reflector* cutting — for the first and only time. He said he wanted it at once, so when Morningside told Miss Quimper that Brigadier Camberley was in a hurry for it, he meant it quite literally.

'As soon as the trap was sprung Camberley left by the glass hatch — which the murderer would be expected to have done — and returned the cutting to its file. Evidently, he knew enough about the system to do that quickly and accurately, and he had to do it. The cutting was on his subject and might be a pointer to him if it were found on Morningside's body or in his office. When he'd replaced it, he went straight down and found Carfrae. That was just before twenty to eight, according to Carfrae, and he stayed till five minutes to. Two minutes later he was in the entrance hall.'

'Stop a minute,' said Toby. 'Why didn't he remove the neg from Morningside's hand — the one you say he used as bait?'

'I don't know, but I've an idea he felt that he oughtn't to disturb the body or the negs or anything else, in case he made the scene look unnatural. No one must be allowed to guess that the murderer had been there at the time Morningside died, and he was afraid he never could recapture the first fine careless rapture. It's said that a lot of murderers are caught because they can't let well alone. And that neg pointed to no one. It was a group of students at some technical college or other.'

'And the *Pirates* neg,' said Toby, 'was found by Camberley when he did the murder?'

'Found by a surprising coincidence, and no doubt destroyed. I dare say he smashed it beyond recognition and added it to the broken negs on the floor. But he must have known, when he found it on Morningside's desk, that he was only just in time. Morningside could have had no interest in the Policemen's Chorus unless he had recognised someone in it. If Camberley hadn't found it, I don't know what he'd have done. He wouldn't have had time to go through the box before he rigged the trap, or the surviving negs afterwards, though he could have checked the remaining boxes at his leisure. But I think he'd have let it go, once Morningside was dead. I saw a copy at Scotland Yard this afternoon, and if I hadn't known it was Camberley, I'd never have recognised it in a hundred years.'

Johnny stopped and relit his pipe. Then he said, 'Miss Quimper's murder was simpler. On the evening he killed her he had been with Silcutt — persuading him to come across with the Dowd story. From Silcutt's office he went, by pure chance, to Morningside's, to look for some pix. He admitted that the next morning, inadvertently, though he didn't mention the time. He overheard Miss Quimper talking to Sally, and he heard her say that Morningside had been looking for a cutting which Camberley had wanted in a hurry. Miss Quimper evidently never understood that Camberley was actually waiting for the cutting in Peex. But one can understand that when he overheard her report of the incident, he was anxious. He had had no idea Morningside had spoken to anyone during those few minutes in Cuts. He didn't know exactly what Morningside had said to Miss Quimper, and he was afraid to let her be questioned closely about it. He knew too that she might remember the *Pirates* neg. So he killed her.'

'Did he really believe,' asked Sally, 'that the doctors wouldn't know she hadn't been pushed off the path?'

'I shouldn't think so. I fancy he hoped to give the impression of an ill-informed murderer — which he wasn't.'

'Anything else?' asked Toby after a minute.

'His general behaviour. He was extremely nice to Sally and me and made things easy for us all along. He wasn't going to arouse our suspicions by obstructing us, and it was to his advantage to keep in with us and hear everything we discovered. He didn't take us very seriously, I imagine, and I'm afraid he was right, because if he hadn't slipped up over *The Pirates*, we'd never have got him at all. And most of the case against him is pure conjecture, you know. We could probably never have proved it.'

Camberley himself must have realised that, thought

Sally. But the merciless certainty in Johnny's eyes, the determination in his face, and most of all, perhaps, his conversion of Wigram, had shown the man he would never get away with it. A jury might find him innocent, but these men would break him by smashing the legend of James Camberley. Forty-eight hours ago she would have found it impossible not to like him. But last night she had seen not James Camberley but William Smith — the man who had battered a middle-aged woman over the head with a poker, and later murdered two tiresome but innocent people to cover his tracks.

'The only person who saw through him,' said Johnny, 'was Michael Knox. I had a drink with him this evening, after I'd been to Scotland Yard. Until a few months ago he admired Camberley enormously — that was why he told him the Dowd story. Then, for no other reason than that he knows his world and has as few illusions as anyone in it, he began to realise that the man was bogus. That, for him, is the unforgivable sin, and that was why he attacked Camberley in the *Reflector*. What's more, he guessed long before I did that Camberley was the murderer.'

There was a long silence. Then Johnny said he was dry and was going down to get some beer.

When the door had shut behind him, Toby stirred restlessly on the sofa and shifted his lame leg. There was a curious expression on his face, and for a minute or two he talked rapidly about nothing in particular. Sally watched him with affectionate amusement while he made up his mind.

At last he said abruptly, 'I wanted to tell you, Sally. It seems incredible, but Selina says she'll marry me. We'll wait a bit, of course, before we announce it. But — well, it seems to have really happened.'

'I'm so glad, Toby, darling,' said Sally. 'You'll be very good for each other.'

'I'm still not at all sure I ought to,' said Toby anxiously. 'With this leg, I mean. I'm not much of a match for anyone as beautiful as she is.'

'I shouldn't worry,' said Sally. 'After all, you might have had some serious disability. You might have been selfish, or bad-tempered, or stupid.'

The colour came into Toby's thin cheeks. He scrambled to his feet, took Sally's hand, and kissed it with an awkward gentleness which she found very touching. Then Johnny came in with the beer, and they drank Toby's and Selina's health.

WANT TO DISCOVER MORE UNCROWNED QUEENS OF CRIME?

SIGN UP TO OUR CRIME CLASSICS NEWSLETTER TO DISCOVER NEW GOLDEN AGE CRIME, RECEIVE EXCLUSIVE CONTENT, AND NEVER-BEFORE PUBLISHED SHORT STORIES, ALL FOR FREE.

FROM THE BELOVED GREATS OF THE GOLDEN AGE TO THE FORGOTTEN GEMS, BEST-KEPT-SECRETS, AND BRAND NEW DISCOVERIES, WE'RE DEVOTED TO CLASSIC CRIME.

IF YOU SIGN UP TODAY, YOU'LL GET:

1. A FREE NOVEL FROM OUR CLASSIC CRIME COLLECTION;

2. EXCLUSIVE INSIGHTS INTO CLASSIC NOVELS AND THEIR AUTHORS; AND,

3. THE CHANCE TO GET COPIES IN ADVANCE OF PUBLICATION.

INTERESTED?

IT TAKES LESS THAN A MINUTE TO SIGN UP, JUST HEAD TO

WWW.CRIMECLASSICS.CO.UK

AND YOUR EBOOK WILL BE SENT TO YOU.

facebook.com/crimeclassics
twitter.com/crimeclassics